Parked outside the Tulips Saloon, Duke drummed the steering wheel

It appeared that there was a party going on inside, one to which he had not been invited. Gathering up his bravado, which had been shamelessly stamped on lately, he strode across the street. He eased open the doors and the smile slipped from his face, his gaze suddenly riveted to the beautiful cake Liberty was about to cut.

The cake was festooned with a tier of pastel pink and blue ribbons, and a silver baby rattle lay beneath it like a shiny announcement of a beautiful, miracle future.

His eyes met Liberty's with horror and heartbreak and in them Duke read the truth: Liberty Wentworth was welcoming a baby into her life. That was the real reason she'd returned to Tulips.

What a faithless would-be-bride she'd turned out to be!

Dear Reader,

Many of you enjoyed the COWBOYS BY THE DOZEN books, and I had fun writing them for you. There are so many more stories in that series that I want to tell, and fortunately, my editor liked my idea of setting some books in a town neighboring Union Junction— Tulips, Texas, a town run by women. The move is truly one from leather to lace, and I loved writing the reverse of the strong-headed, strong-hearted men in COWBOYS BY THE DOZEN. Mainly, I loved being able to revisit old friends and make some new ones. I hope you will enjoy this three-book series— welcome to a town peopled with citizens who really love each other and understand that friendships are one of the most important parts of life.

Much love to you all,

Tina Leonard

TINA LEONARD
My Baby, My Bride

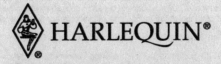

HARLEQUIN®

TORONTO • NEW YORK • LONDON
AMSTERDAM • PARIS • SYDNEY • HAMBURG
STOCKHOLM • ATHENS • TOKYO • MILAN • MADRID
PRAGUE • WARSAW • BUDAPEST • AUCKLAND

ISBN-13: 978-0-373-75133-4
ISBN-10:   0-373-75133-8

MY BABY, MY BRIDE

www.eHarlequin.com

Printed in U.S.A.

ABOUT THE AUTHOR

Tina Leonard loves to laugh, which is one of the many reasons she loves writing Harlequin American Romance books. In another lifetime Tina thought she would be single and an East Coast fashion buyer forever. The unexpected happened when Tina met Tim again after many years—she hadn't seen him since they'd attended school together from first through eighth grade. They married, and now Tina keeps a close eye on her school-age children's friends! Lisa and Dean keep their mother busy with soccer, gymnastics and horseback riding. They are proud of their mom's "kissy books" and eagerly help her any way they can. Tina hopes that readers will enjoy the love of family she writes about in her books. Recently a reviewer wrote, "Leonard had a wonderful sense of the ridiculous," which Tina loved so much she wants it for her epitaph. Right now, however, she's focusing on her wonderful life and writing a lot more romance! You can visit her at www.tinaleonard.com.

Books by Tina Leonard

HARLEQUIN AMERICAN ROMANCE

This book is dedicated to
Kathleen Scheibling and Paula Eykelhof.
Many thanks for the wonders of my career.

To Lisa and DeanO, my best little friends.
I love you.

And to my Gal Pals, and the Scandalous Ladies
and wonderful friend Georgia Haynes—
what marvelous friends and teachers
you have been to me.

Chapter One

"Most of the memorable women, fiction or nonfiction, have been willing to raise a little hell."
—Liberty Wentworth, throwing caution to the wind

It was Ladies Only Day in the Tulips Saloon in Tulips, Texas, but Sheriff Duke Forrester pitched the heavy glass-and-wood doors open anyway, drawing a gasp from the crowd of women clustered around something in the center of the room.

The ladies were, as usual, hiding something from him. In this town, named by women, and mostly run by women—it was true that behind every good woman there was a woman who'd taught her everything she knew—he had learned to outmaneuver both the younger and the older population of ladies bent on intrigues of the social, sexual and conspiratorial varieties.

"I heard," he said, his voice a no-nonsense drawl, "that Liberty Wentworth was back in town. You ladies wouldn't know anything about that, would you?"

Every one of them shook her head as the women tightened their circle. It was, he decided, almost an engraved invitation for him to storm their protective clutch and find out what they were up to. By now, they should know he was on to them. Oh, he'd let them have their way when they'd wanted to name the town cafeteria a saloon—they said a saloon sounded so much more dramatic to tourists who wanted that "old west experience." But he wouldn't let them have their way this time.

Liberty Wentworth, his ex-fiancée, was trying to keep her return to Tulips a secret, he was sure, with a backing of blue-haired friends. Some silver-haired friends, too, depending on what Holt, the resident hairdresser, was mixing up for his clients. Duke was pretty certain Holt's colorful creations were a reflection of the man's current mood, but the ladies loved him, calling him "sympathetic" to their cause.

Mostly, their cause was outwitting the sheriff,

and this was plot number ninety-nine, give or take a few. Duke grinned, edging a foot closer to the ladies. Their faces grew worried with round-eyed concern.

"Now, this is Ladies Only Day," Helen Granger said sternly. "Sheriff, you know that means no gentlemen in here."

"Considering there are, what, maybe ten men in this town of fifty residents, I have to take exception to the rule. I think you ladies just like one day when you know I personally won't be allowed in."

"Is one day of sisterhood too much to ask?" Helen demanded. "One day of female bonding in our saloon? Hentalk can't interest you that much, Sheriff."

The hentalk comment gave them away, Duke decided, craning his neck to see what they were hiding. Women never called their chatter "hentalk," and if a man called it that, he'd lose his hat from the gale-force wind of them yelling it off his head. "I notice Holt is excluded from The Rule," he said silkily.

"Well, Holt's different," Pansy Trifle explained. "You know he is. Not like yourself at all. Not so *manly*," she said, sucking up and trying to flatter his ego.

Ha. He had no ego. Liberty Wentworth had taken care of his ego six months ago when she'd left him at the altar, her little feet in high-heeled white shoes running as fast as they could away from him, her veil flying behind her like a banner ribbon of surrender to freedom.

"All right, ladies," he said, gently moving Pansy to one side. "Let's see what you're up to this time."

Immediately after he'd parted the women, he wished he hadn't felt such an urge to play his *manly* role of plot-buster. Because there in the center of the sheltering circle of her friends was Liberty Wentworth, the blond bombshell who had detonated his heart, still possessing the face of an angel and wearing the white wedding gown of his never-ending fantasies. Nightmares, really. His heart began an uncomfortable pounding as she stared up into his eyes. If life were fair, he'd whip out his handcuffs right now and snap them on her fragile wrists so she'd be completely at his mercy.

Unfortunately, as much as the thought of Liberty in sexual bondage was a highly desirable situation, the ladies would beat him to death with parasols, tea trays and opinions. He had only one course of action left to him, one source of honor for his masculine pride.

He turned on his boot heel and walked out the

door, surrendering to the sanctity of Ladies Only Day and hiding the sudden pain in his chest. Liberty was clearly planning on marrying another man, in the dress she'd worn to their non-wedding, no less. The woman was a serial marital tornado, he decided, putting himself in a better mood by pitying the next poor sap who was going to get his heart squashed by her now.

He despised Ladies Only Day with a passion.

Five minutes later, Duke was safely corralled inside his office at the jailhouse. It was dark and quiet, and that was good. He needed a moment or two to regroup, and to curse privately.

"Howdy, Sheriff."

Duke put his hand up, warding off the greeting from the jail cell's erstwhile occupant. "Not now, Mr. Parsons." Duke sat heavily in the worn leather chair he'd inherited from the previous occupant of the sheriff's position, Mrs. Gaines. Mr. Parsons's silky-haired golden retriever, Jimbo, came to lay his head on the corner of Duke's desk, giving him a soulful, sympathetic gaze. Actually, the damn dog was Duke's, and actually, her name was Molly. But about the time Liberty decided to jilt him, Molly had also jilted him, leaving him for the warm, frequent, measured stroking Mr. Parsons offered her. Since

Mr. Parsons had once owned a dog named Jimbo, whom he'd adored, Molly had undergone a psychic personality transformation—or a theoretical sex change—and become Jimbo. The rest was history. Duke stared at his meekly sympathetic dog, who was really a traitor in gorgeous fur come back to taunt him. Much like Liberty. *Traitor.* "All females are traitors," he stated flatly to Mr. Parsons.

"Not necessarily," Mr. Parsons replied. He'd finished making his bed and was picking up a broom to sweep out his cell. The cell door was open because Mr. Parsons was a volunteer occupant. He kept his cell cleaner than most folks kept their homes, so Duke had quit arguing with him about the fact that eventually he'd have to give up the cell for some vagrant or deserving troublemaker. Mr. Parsons had also deemed himself Duke's secretary, so the man was of some use, even if his messages were indecipherable more often than not. "Mrs. Parsons was no traitor, though I often suspected she spied on me for the KGB."

Duke rubbed his forehead under his hatband. "Liberty is a spy," he said, jumping on the conspiracy theory because he was tired and annoyed. And heartbroken. "She's a spy for the TSG."

"Tulips Saloon girls?"

"Tulips Saloon *Gang*. Believe me, they are a gang."

"Women tend to run as a pack," Mr. Parsons observed. "And that's where the fun is usually to be found. I'd run with their gang if they'd let me."

Duke leaned back in his chair and closed his eyes. Molly-Jimbo's head moved from his desk to his leg, and she gave an empathetic tweet of shared misery, which he appreciated so much that he put his hand down to enjoy the feeling of her silky ear between his fingers. "Just like Liberty's hair," he murmured.

"Pardon?" Mr. Parsons said.

Duke ignored him. Truth was, the old man was mostly quiet, and he had Duke's dog, and Duke figured that was as practical a reason as any to let good company hang around. Mainly, he didn't want to be completely alone with his thoughts, which always returned in ragged fashion to Liberty Wentworth.

LIBERTY ADJUSTED the flowing folds of her wedding gown and told her racing heart to quiet itself after Duke's departure. "Duke only got *half* the surprise."

Helen and Pansy fluttered around her. "A man doesn't need to be overwhelmed with information," Pansy said. "I think the sheriff took in all he could handle for the moment."

"He asked for it," Helen said crossly. "If a man walks through those doors on our special day, then he's asking to get an education in women's ways."

The other ten or so women in the room nodded. One handed Liberty a tissue; another went and loaded up a plate of cookies that had been brought over from the neighboring town of Union Junction by Valentine Jefferson. She was the owner of the bakery there, and had given them the idea to start a Ladies Only Day. Her Men's Only Day in Union Junction—a celebration of males, masculinity and fatherhood—had been a big success and had done much to boost the morale of the town.

It had seemed like such a good idea at the time, Liberty thought to herself. A day just for women, where they could bond with each other and share their most personal triumphs and disappointments.

She had come here today just for this brand of womanly comfort. "I'm sorry," Liberty said. "I've put all of you in a bad spot now."

"Nonsense," Pansy said, her posture stout and determined. "As far as Sheriff Duke is concerned, we are always in a bad spot. We *like* it that way!"

Liberty smiled at her friend's pluck.

"That's right," Helen agreed. "We're determined to go out of this world raising hell, and Duke makes such an excellent foil for our objectives."

That announcement seemed to center the group because the ladies stopped hovering and fluttering. They sat and reached for teacups and sweets. Liberty felt like neither eating nor drinking.

Of course, that had something to do with being pregnant with Duke's child, the other half of the shock he would eventually endure. Dread filled her.

"Do you need a toddy, dear?" Pansy asked. "A good, sweet lemonade?"

Since it was a hot September in Texas, lemonade would normally be a refreshing treat. But not today—not since Duke had discovered she'd returned. Since seeing his handsome face, Liberty felt her stomach wouldn't accept a thing.

"Maybe I should talk to him," she said.

Valentine looked at her. "There is a time for talking, especially with someone as stubborn as Duke. I married a stubborn man and truthfully, catching Crockett was the hard part. After that, it's been a lot of fun." She smiled with encouragement.

Even with the support of all these wonderful ladies, Liberty felt her courage begin to drain out of her. "I really didn't have catching Duke on my mind, since I technically returned him to the wild on our wedding day."

"There is that," Helen said. She sat down, shifting her black glasses on her nose and peering at

Liberty. "It's amazing how that wedding dress still fits you, as far along as you are." Frowning, she touched the delicate lace. "I'm not certain the waist can be let out, dear, once you start gaining…once baby starts growing more. We're pushing it at seven months, and I do believe it's now or never for your lovely gown."

An awkward silence fell over the room. Liberty stood. "This is my problem, and I've made everyone feel that it's theirs. I'm going to walk down to the jail and talk to Duke."

"You should change first, dear," Pansy observed mildly. "Duke would probably be more receptive to you when you aren't wearing white."

"She didn't mean that the way it sounded, Libby," Helen hurried to say, but Liberty shook her head.

"It's all right." Hugging Pansy to melt the expression of dismay on her elderly friend's face, she said, "I'll wear black. That ought to suit his mood since he clearly thinks I'm the evil witch of Tulips."

"Black is sexy," Valentine noted.

"Yes, but I don't think he's in the mood to see me as sexy. To him, I'm the villainess of this play," Liberty said, "and I can't blame him. Unzip me, if you don't mind, Helen."

"Such a pretty gown," Helen murmured.

Liberty could feel the woman's fingers tremble at the delicate shell buttons and zipper at the back. "It's just that Duke's so strong," she said to the room at large, as all the women watched the fantasy wedding gown coming undone with sad, wistful eyes. "He's very opinionated. I got scared," she said, trying to apologize, or at least explain her actions to the women who cared so much about her. She could feel their heartbreak and their concern. Of course, she'd had no idea she was pregnant at the time. Would she still have jilted Duke?

"Strong is good," one of the younger women murmured. "I like a strong man."

"Mmm. John Wayne," someone else said.

"But a man can be *too* opinionated," Valentine said, and Liberty felt better.

"Depends on where and how he decides to express his opinions," someone commented, drawing a few giggles, though not from Liberty, Pansy, Helen or Valentine.

The heavy doors of the Tulips Saloon crashed open. All the ladies gasped, not the least because of the fabulous stained-glass design of hot pink and red tulips that adorned the door, but mainly from the shock of being startled from their conversation—again.

"Liberty!" Duke's voice could have drowned

out a cannon's boom. She whirled to look at him, holding her hands to the sweetheart neckline of the dress so it wouldn't fall from her shoulders.

She raised her chin, not about to answer him meekly. "You snarled?"

"We need to talk," he said, his arms crossed.

"*Need* has never been one of my favorite words," she said. "I prefer *would like to,* or even *should.*"

"Phrased nicely," Pansy said, bobbing her head so that her spectacles danced. "'We should talk' would sound ever so much more chivalrous."

"I'll wait for you outside." He tipped his hat to the room and left.

Liberty looked at her friends. "That is the definition of strong."

"Well," Valentine said, "he is upset."

"He does need some sugar on that temper of his," someone suggested.

"Of course, he was devastated when she left," another matron sympathized.

"Well," Helen said with a sigh, "go change, honey. Let him cool his heels a minute. I'll tell him you'll be right out, and maybe that will settle him." She picked up a delicate teacup, poured some fresh tea in it and bravely headed outside to offer it to the sheriff.

Liberty went into a back room and slipped out

of the beautiful gown with Valentine's help. Valentine hung the dress for her, covering it in plastic. Even beneath the cover, the dress shimmered with hope and dreams of happiness. Liberty had sewn every single one of those sequins and crystal beads herself, and had cut the satiny fabric with trembling fingers while Pansy and Helen helped her keep it from snagging or getting dirty. That dress had been a labor of love on all their parts.

"The ladies say he really is a teddy bear," Valentine said.

"He is," Liberty agreed, "when he's not being a horse's ass. You don't get one without the other with Duke."

Valentine giggled. "I heard his brother, Zach, is the same way."

"Zach may be worse. Although Pepper takes the cake," Liberty said. "Little sister knows exactly how to tame those brothers of hers."

"Where is Pepper, anyway?" Valentine asked, carefully smoothing the plastic covering the dream dress.

"I don't know. Off somewhere, being a wild woman." She smiled as she pulled on jeans and a loose white sweater. "I think the fact that Pepper and I were best friends growing up gives me insight into the family. Zach and I were close, almost as much as Pepper and I were. But not Duke. I think I fell in love with him when I was five years old. I was watching him catch tadpoles, and I remember thinking he could do anything." He had been her hero.

A part of her still thought he was.

She shook her head as she stepped back into her high-heeled wedding shoes. There wasn't going to be a wedding but she might as well wear them, even if they might be the color of sin in Duke's eyes. The heels would make her a little taller when talking to him—and a little sexier, despite her pregnancy.

"Your shoes and sweater match," Valentine said. "You look so pretty, Liberty. No one would ever guess you're seven months pregnant. I hope you don't mind me saying so."

Liberty smiled. "Thanks."

"I'm going to head back to Union Junction. I'll give your dress to Helen and Pansy." She hugged Liberty. "In the meantime, good luck with Duke."

Pansy poked her head around the door. "Duke says he's gotten a call and he's got to leave, so you'd best hurry, dear."

Liberty hugged Valentine again and followed Pansy out, waving to her friends who watched her depart with some concern. Outside the saloon,

Duke stood on the sidewalk, sexy as all get out and clearly disgruntled.

"I have to go," he said. "I have a call. But we *should* talk."

Noting he'd used the ladies' more courteous phrasing, she gave him points for trying and nodded. "All right."

"You can ride with me if you like." He eyed her wedding shoes. "Although we'll be going into the country on a family crisis call."

"Who is it?" She followed Duke with quick steps as he strode away.

"The Carmines. Mrs. Carmine says her husband left last night and she wants someone to talk to. She thinks he may have gotten lost."

"Again," Liberty murmured. Bug Carmine frequently departed to his fields with a bottle of whiskey and a shotgun. The shotgun was in case he saw a deer or duck he wanted, though in his ten years of disappearing, he'd never brought home food nor trophy. People suspected he couldn't see more than five feet in front of him. His disappearance upset Mrs. Carmine after a few days. She would call someone to fetch him from the five hundred acres he could hide himself in, and he'd come home sheepishly, bottle empty but shotgun still loaded.

They got in Duke's truck. He glanced over at her, and Liberty's nerves tightened.

"So," he said, "who's the lucky guy?"

Chapter Two

"There is no lucky guy," Liberty said. "You should know that better than anyone."

He scowled. Why had he asked? No matter the answer, it was bound to hurt. But she wouldn't have been wearing the wedding gown if she wasn't intending to marry another man.

It was killing him.

"No second chances from me," he said. "I'm not asking twice."

He felt her astonishment. "I'm not asking you to ask me, if you're referring to marriage." Her posture stiffened. "Duke, my leaving had more to do with me than you. I got scared. I wasn't ready. Even I didn't know I was a predestined runaway bride. It just happened, silly as that seems."

"If it was any woman other than you who'd done that, I'd think they were a little loose in the skull," he said. "But being loosey-goosey is sort of your way. I think it's what attracts me to you."

Of course, there were a lot of other things that attracted him to her. Right now he could smell her perfume. It smelled wonderful, reminding him of the scent of her skin. The memory worked him over. "I think you weren't convinced."

"Of what?"

"You weren't convinced that you couldn't live without me. Since we never really dated but made love twice—in one afternoon—you probably were unconvinced that I was husband material."

"I don't think that was it. But let's not examine it too much. If we try to overanalyze it, we might figure something out, and I don't want to. It's in the past."

He didn't like that. "Completely?"

"Not exactly," she said.

"Aha! You did like sleeping with me!"

"I never said I didn't," she said tartly. "That was the one really good thing about you."

"What the hell does that mean?" He couldn't decide if he was gratified or insulted. "Liberty, when I asked you to marry me, you said yes. I assumed there was something about me you liked beyond the bedroom."

"The field," Liberty murmured, "and then a closet."

"It was awesome. I never knew a woman could be so flexible."

"Duke!" She sighed. "Good sex doesn't a marriage make."

"It makes something," he said, "and in my book, it makes something good."

"Yes, well—" Her voice drifted away. "I want something more solid than sexual desire. That fades away over time."

He turned into the Carmines' drive. "Like what? A written promise that I'll always want you enough to make love to you in a closet?"

"Yes." Liberty nodded. "And that you'll never try to rule me, or boss me, or overwhelm me with your personality. You're very chauvinistic in some ways, Duke."

He laughed. "Not me. That would be my brother, Zach."

She shook her head. "Zach was always the gentleman. The girls love him. You were always the autocratic one."

"That's why I'm sheriff," he said happily. "It's an autocracy." He stopped the engine. "You've been hanging around those little blue-haired friends of yours too much. Any day now I expect them to bring out their suffragette banners."

"That's not very nice, Duke Forrester. Shame on you."

He smiled, appreciating the sensation of being the bad boy with a bad girl. "I couldn't boss you even if I wanted to, Liberty Wentworth. You're far too unquantifiable for that." Leaning over, he brushed her lips with his. "Of course, I'll always be bullheaded enough to take what's mine."

"That's it," Liberty said, getting out of the truck, "you flunked the test."

"Poor testing parameters, if you ask me." He took her arm, helping her to the porch. "You and I were made for each other. We're like an odd shape, not meant to fit another puzzle on the planet."

"Sounds dreadful." Liberty knocked on the door. "Mrs. Carmine! Are you home? It's Liberty Wentworth!"

"I believe that's my job," Duke said to her. "And Sheriff Duke Forrester!"

"Sometimes it's easier for women to talk to women. Especially about things like husbands that run off for days."

He crooked an eyebrow at her. "One day, our last name is going to be the same, and then we can stand on Mrs. Carmine's front porch and just holler 'It's the Forresters!'"

"Sounds like a movie title. Maybe it is. It was probably a bad one, too," she said as Mrs. Carmine opened the door.

"No way. Everything about the two of us together is good," Duke said as Liberty hugged Mrs. Carmine.

"How are you doing?" Liberty asked the elderly lady.

"I'm fine." She smiled bravely. "I'm just lonely. Would you mind fetching my husband home?" she asked Duke.

It would be a chore searching all the acreage, but one he'd done many times. "*A pleasure,*" he said, interpreting Liberty's glare to mean *be gracious.* "We'll go right now. Don't you worry about a thing, Mrs. Carmine. We'll tell Bug it's time to get home."

She nodded. "Thank you. It's good to see you, Liberty," she said, her voice quavering. "If I'd known how men like to disappear, I probably wouldn't have married Bug, as much as I hate to say it."

Great. That's all I need—a little help from the "Wish I Hadn't" club. "Now, Mrs. Carmine," Duke said patiently, "you know you love Bug."

"Bug is a pain in my ass," she declared. "Like

a child, always running off." She looked at Liberty. "You're lucky Duke is such a stalwart sort."

Duke enjoyed the blush pinkening Liberty's face. It was good for Liberty to know that other women considered him a catch!

"Of course, stalwart can be boring," Mrs. Carmine said with a frown. "If I was your age again, I'd run off with an Italian lover or a Russian circus performer first. Then I might settle down. *Might*."

Liberty blinked. "Let me fix you a cup of hot tea, Mrs. Carmine."

"No." A sigh so deep it made her pinafore rise escaped her. "You just go find my Bug before I get the urge to squash him."

Liberty hugged the older woman, then walked out the front door Duke held open for her.

"Now don't go getting any ideas," Duke said. "It's well-known that the Carmines married very young."

"Her words are food for thought, though," Liberty said.

"Try a diet," Duke said. "Some foods aren't healthy for you."

Liberty got in the truck. "Then again, sometimes the food you like most is the least healthy for you."

He turned to look at her before grabbing her

shoulders and kissing her hard. "How's that for an appetizer?" he asked after he'd thoroughly ravaged her mouth.

She raised her chin and gave him a haughty look. "So good I prefer to skip the main course."

He rammed his hat down on his head, not sure what to say to that. What was wrong with her? Women didn't push him away as hard as Liberty was doing. Driving down the hill into the back pasture, he considered his options where Liberty was concerned.

He didn't appear to have many.

"Duke, when do you run for reelection?"

The change of subject startled him. "I don't really run. No one else wants the job. I've always been a shoo-in."

"When does that happen?"

"I suppose the elections are this month. I hadn't really thought about it." He began to scan the landscape for Bug. "You look on that side, I'll look over here."

He thought about her question and idly wondered what had brought her back to town. "Are you running?"

She looked at him. "From you?"

"For sheriff," he stated flatly, his jaw tightening. Did she have to bring that up again?

"Oh, no. I heard your brother Zach was. Then I heard your sister Pepper was, but that's silly. Pepper's not here."

His jaw untightened and went slack. "Where did you hear that?"

"At the saloon."

"They haven't told me."

"Actually, what I think I heard is that the ladies have decided to petition them onto the ballot."

"The ladies?" Duke demanded. "By that you mean the little group that's constantly scheming." He was slightly hurt, he had to admit. The "ladies" always conspired against him, but it was usually in a somewhat delightful spirit that he indulged. They were, after all, much older than he and deserved his respect.

But petitioning his siblings onto a ballot to run against him didn't sound like something he cared to indulge. He kept looking for Bug, trying to ignore the hammering in his heart.

"*All* the ladies," she clarified. "At least the ones who were in attendance at today's Ladies Only Day."

"I knew that was a bad idea. If the men had been there, the gang would have been soundly overruled." He scratched his chin, aware that he was beginning to sound truculent. He softened his tone. "You still haven't told me what you were doing wearing the dress you were supposed to wear to our wedding. I have fond memories of you trying it on and letting me button those tiny little buttons."

He had taken his sweet time doing so, enjoying touching her and looking down at her bare shoulders. She was the smoothest, softest thing he'd ever seen.

"The ladies were trying to convince me that it was a good idea to marry you," Liberty said. "I had a weak moment."

"Ouch."

"No! I didn't mean that. I meant that I allowed them to coerce me into trying it on." She put a hand on his arm. "Duke, it wasn't you as much as it was me, really and truly."

"You spend too much time around women, listening to them gripe about their men," he said gruffly, "and it scared you."

"No, frankly just the thought of marrying you spooked me." She sighed. "You can't blame them. I had my own doubts."

"I'm not so terrible," he complained.

She turned away. "You'll be wonderful for the right woman."

"You are the right woman!" he roared. "Or at least you would be if you'd act right."

"Duke," she said, "we'd end up like the Carmines."

"Only you'd be the one running off. Even Mrs. Carmine said I'm stalwart." He was proud of that. "By the way, you still look good enough to eat in that dress. It always reminds me of a big, fluffy piece of Ms. Pansy's divinity when I see you in it."

"Ugh. I'm not sure that's what it was supposed to evoke."

"I like dessert, so the dress was perfect, in my opinion."

"There he is," Liberty said, pointing.

Duke slowed the truck as he saw the old man sitting propped against a tree, watching ducks fly overhead. His rifle was on the ground next to him but the elderly man didn't have a hand on it. He appeared to be watching the wedge of ducks as they flew, perfectly content to enjoy the silence and the heat of the day. "He doesn't look ready to go home."

"You tell him," Liberty said. "I'm not in a position to tell someone they should return home."

"You got that right," Duke said, "and I might remind you, based on the popular opinion of my stalwartness, you should tell your lady friends that their idea to write Zach and Pepper into the ballot hurt my feelings."

Liberty laughed. Then she saw the seriousness of his face as he parked the truck. "Did it really?"

"Yes, damn it." He switched off the engine, keeping an eye on Mr. Carmine. "How would you feel if you knew all your townfolk that you'd sworn to serve and protect were always conspiring against you?"

"It's not actually against you," Liberty said, but Duke waved her comforting words aside.

"Sure it is. They've got some bee in their bonnets over something. Like I haven't given in to them enough. They wanted to change the name of the town to reflect the Dutch ancestry of the settlers, so I agreed. They wanted to change the name of a perfectly good establishment to make it more of a tourist attraction, and I agreed to that, with great reservation. Now they're trying to run me out by writing in my siblings' names—one of whom hasn't been here in a year—with their little wizened hands. Judases!" He frowned. "Or would that be Jezebels?"

"Oh, gosh." Liberty got out of the truck. "Duke, come on. We've got a job to do."

He got out, his heart heavy. What was the matter with all the females in his world? Clearly none of them cared that he was so easy to get along with.

It wasn't fair.

"Hello, Mr. Carmine," he said.

"Howdy, Sheriff," Bug said, not surprised to see him at all. "Nice day, isn't it?" He nodded to Liberty. "Glad to see you back in town, girl."

Liberty sat next to him. She picked up his bottle, which looked empty and probably had been for some time. From her jeans pocket, she pulled out a package of spearmint gum, and they each had a piece. Duke raised an eyebrow, watching this silent communication.

"Mrs. Carmine is wondering about you," Duke said.

Bug looked back at the sky as if searching for the ducks he'd been watching before. But they were long gone and only small white clouds trailed across the blue in cumulus strings. Bug's gaze came to rest on Duke. "How's your jail, Sheriff?"

"It's a jail," Duke said. "And occupied," he continued quickly, in case Bug was looking for a place to stay. "Mr. Parsons is still in residence."

Bug nodded. "Marriage is a jail, and I'm still in residence, too."

Liberty shot a worried glance at Duke. He remained silent. Maybe his powers of communication weren't quite what he'd thought they'd been.

Liberty stood, putting her hand out to Mr.

Carmine. After a moment, Bug took her hand and lifted himself to his feet, giving all appearances of using Liberty's strength as emotional support. Duke watched as the two of them headed to the truck. Bug silently settled himself into the back seat of the double cab. Liberty nodded at him, telling him they were ready to go, so he got behind the wheel and drove back to the ranch house.

Mrs. Carmine came out onto the porch, her face lit with a gentle smile. Bug got out of the truck, and walked toward the house, where he was enveloped in a big hug he seemed happy to return. The two of them went inside the house arm in arm and closed the front door.

Duke blinked. Checking the back seat, he saw Bug's shotgun and empty whiskey bottle.

"He won't need the gun 'til next time," Liberty said. "Why don't you just keep it with you at the jail for now? He'll come get it soon enough."

He didn't understand any of what had just happened. But Liberty seemed to, and he was happy to take her suggestion. "What happens now?"

She shrugged. "Now Mrs. Carmine ignores that he went away because she loves him, and he ignores the fact that he's unhappy because it's not her fault."

What a prison. A curse, maybe. Like something out of a Grimm's fairy tale. Duke plucked at the steering wheel. Maybe Liberty was on to something where they were concerned, though he was hard-pressed to admit it.

Still, he didn't want her to ever think marriage to him was a jail, though Mr. Parsons seemed to like his own prison well enough. "Ye gods, you people are hard to live with," he said, and Liberty looked at him.

"So?" she asked. "Your conclusion?"

"That you're right," he said slowly. "There really is no happy ending."

"I think not," Liberty said, "which is a very scary thought."

"Damn," Duke said. "I need to get home and feed my dog." He started the engine, glad to have an excuse to hurry back to town.

"I thought Mr. Parsons took care of Molly-Jimbo."

"He feeds her peanuts as a snack," Duke said righteously. "I want to make certain I head him off at the pass."

"Does she like the peanuts?"

"Molly likes anything that comes from a human hand."

"Then what's the problem?" Liberty asked.

"I don't like it. A dog should eat dry dog food."

Liberty raised a brow. "Duke, do you ever bend the rules?"

"No," Duke said, surprised. "If I did, I wouldn't be sheriff, would I? At least not a very good one."

Liberty turned her head to look out the opposite window. "I suppose not."

They rode in silence until they reached the town square.

"Please drop me off at the Tulips Saloon," Liberty said.

"It should be closed. No one will be there."

"I have a key," Liberty said.

"A key?"

"Yes. Of course. I am one of the co-owners of the saloon," she said. "Along with Pansy and Helen and a few others, as you very well know. It was our gift to ourselves, a woman-owned business."

"And a questionable one at that," Duke grumbled, griping because he knew full-well that the ladies had been catching tourists who came to town with their stained-glass-decorated monument to femininity and womanhood. "I just thought that perhaps since you'd left town, maybe you'd given up your key."

She looked at him for a long moment, long enough to make his heart shrivel. God, how he wanted to kiss her again, kiss her the way they used to kiss, without worry or hurry or anything more than intense pleasure on their minds.

"I guess you were the only person who thought I'd never come back," Liberty finally said. She got out of the truck and closed the door, not looking back. The door to the saloon opened for her, and Helen and Pansy peered out at him before snatching Liberty inside and slamming the door.

Heaven only knew how he'd become the villain.

Chapter Three

Duke was proud of three things in his life: his family, his job and his reputation. He loved his sister, Pepper, and his brother, Zach, so it hurt that they might be part of the blue-haired angels' plan to oust him from the vocation of which he was most proud. All of this directly impacted his reputation, which was bad enough. The root cause of the problem, he realized, was the woman he loved.

He had a plan for dealing with Liberty Wentworth-who-should-be-Forrester-by-now. A taste of her own medicine was what she needed. If he could straighten her bent ways, then all the rest of the crooked line that had become his life would return to being straight-as-an-arrow predictable as the road to the Forrester homestead, on which he was now driving with his traitorous brother.

"Maybe," Zach said, watching Duke glare out

the windshield, "you should talk to the ladies. They'll have insights into your female issues."

Duke pinned him with the glare. "Zach, do not violate the bachelor code."

"Is there one?"

"Hell, yes. Bachelors only commiserate with each other. They never, ever side with the enemy."

"Since when are women the enemy? I like them," Zach said. "I've got two dates this weekend."

"I've got the Tulips Saloon Gang banded together against me with their dolly faces and their innocently spindly frames. I need backup, please, so don't give me any more advice like that. It just doesn't help."

"Spindly?" Zach repeated with a laugh.

"Yes," Duke said, "how can anyone put up a good fight against such frail and fragile creatures?"

Zach shook his head.

"And I want to know how much a part of their newest plot you are," Duke said indignantly. "And don't act like it's news to you, because they've already told me about The Plot."

His brother grinned. "We just think you might need a vacation, Duke. Of the honeymoon variety. Take some time off. Start a family."

"Did I ask anyone's advice?" Duke abruptly braked to a stop in front of the house, sending up clouds of dust. He turned to face his brother for dramatic impact so Zach would know he'd really stepped over the line this time. "I don't want to start a family, thank you. And I like my job a lot. It's never boring." He thought about that for a moment. "In fact, it's downright exciting, a cross between *Peyton Place* and *Petticoat Junction*."

Zach slapped him on the back. "It was Pepper's idea."

Duke gestured toward the old house. "Pepper doesn't even live here!"

"Actually, she does now," Zach said, pointing to an upstairs window where their little sister waved at them with something that looked vaguely like a butterfly net.

"Did she come home to hunt insects?" Duke asked.

"I believe that was a Victoria's Secret undergarment," Zach said, amused. "Not that I'm surprised you didn't know."

"Why would she wave that out the window?"

Zach laughed. "Because she's crazy and it was what she was holding at the time we pulled up. She's unpacking her suitcase, dummy. How 'bout you go give her a proper brotherly greeting and act like you're happy she's back after all these years?"

"But selfishly, I'm not," Duke said, following Zach, though he knew in his heart he was glad. "If the only reason she's come home is to conspire and plot—"

"Duke, everybody conspires and plots with Helen and Pansy and the rest of them. Even you do. So let it go."

Duke didn't like that, but there was a bit of truth to the comment, so he did what he wanted to do, which was take the stairs three at a time and grab his sister in a bear hug. "I'm so glad you're home," he said. "You can cook my dinner."

Pepper laughed and gave him a smart kick in the shin. "No deal. You are cooking mine. *I'm* the weary traveler."

She looked anything but weary. "You were gone too long," he told her.

"I was here for your wedding," she said. "February wasn't that long ago."

He frowned at her. "I meant…you know what? You're as bad as Zach. You just want to argue!"

She put her arm through his. "I like arguing with you. Your face gets all red. And you make such an easy target because you have so many opinions."

He shook his head, liking how she linked her arm through his and led him down the stairs. Sometimes Liberty was soft with him like this, too, and he always melted for women who knew how to work him. Not that that was particularly a good thing. A man had to watch women who plotted against him. Even his dog knew he was a softie.

"Please tell me you didn't return to run for my office."

"I didn't, although something was mentioned to me about it, I will admit," Pepper said. "But I have bigger things in mind."

"Great," Duke said. "Tulips needs fresh blood. Where are you going?"

"Into town," she said, grabbing a gaily wrapped present off the entryway table.

"Hey, I'll drive you," he said. "Bye, Zach. Thanks for the pep talk."

Zach laughed, appreciating the sarcasm. "Any time."

Molly, who had come along for the ride, leaped into the truck bed, a blur of golden beauty. "She loves you," Pepper said.

"When it suits her," Duke said, starting the engine. "Who's the present for?"

"Someone special," Pepper replied, with a teasing smile. "Drive and mind your own business."

"Not as if I won't know eventually. There are no secrets in this town."

Pepper laughed. "The hell there aren't. Tulips is charmingly secretive."

He frowned. "I've always found it to be annoyingly busybody."

"Duke," Pepper said, "one day you're going to have to accept where you live. And the people you live with."

"I do. I'm the sheriff, aren't I?"

"This is a woman's town. You should feel lucky. You get good food, good gossip and lots of drama. All the ladies suck up to you."

"Not anymore. Liberty ruined it," he said. "Now all the women treat me as if I contain a polar charge. They bounce away any time I get close." He frowned. "It's not fair. Zach has two dates this weekend, and all I want is one."

"Really?"

"Yeah," Duke said, not wanting to talk about it anymore. He wasn't going to get the date he wanted, so that left him with the option of moping or getting over it, and he always preferred to get over whatever needed getting over. "But I've got a plan to straighten out Miss Liberty."

"You do?"

He was pleased by the surprise in his sister's tone. "Yes. She wants to play hard-to-get. I will be harder-to-get. And I may even date other women, if necessary."

"To make her jealous?"

He scratched at his chin, not certain Liberty *would* be jealous. "Just to let her know she's not the only girl around."

"Oh. Okay."

As they pulled up in front of the Tulips Saloon, a melodic sound tinkled through the truck, sounding very much like a wind-up lullaby. Duke listened for a moment, unable to place where the sound was coming from. "Your cell phone?"

Pepper hesitated a moment. "It sounded like a cell phone, didn't it?" She smoothed the fancy pink-and-blue ribbon on the big box in her lap.

"You going to answer it?"

"I don't think so. Not right now."

The music stopped, so Duke shrugged. "Well, they'll call again."

"No doubt they will," Pepper murmured. "Thanks for the ride." She kissed his cheek and got out of the truck. He waited while she patted Molly, who then decided to follow Pepper into the saloon, much to his chagrin. The dog was completely faithless, a Pied Piper to whomever petted her.

A moment later, Pansy and Helen disappeared inside the doors of the saloon, also carrying wrapped presents. Then in his rearview mirror he saw Valentine pushing a white wicker pram on huge wheels and walking alongside a rangy cowboy—the kind who made the girls squirm and swoon at rodeos. He carried a large cake in his big arms. They, too, went into the Tulips Saloon.

"It isn't Ladies Only Day," Duke declared to no one but himself. He drummed the steering wheel, straightening when Holt the hairdresser also went inside. It appeared that there was a party, one to which he had not been invited, which gnawed at his already rough feelings. What in the hell was going on in there?

There were more arrivals, including Mr. Parsons and Mr. Carmine, who looked around with surreptitious glances to make certain they weren't seen before slipping inside as well. Duke blinked. They hadn't been carrying presents, but... The Plot! Of course, The Plot. The townspeople really were working to unseat him! "What did I do to deserve this?" he asked himself. There was nothing for him to do but slink back to his jailhouse and try to ignore the fact that it was utterly empty for once. He could clean out a filing cabinet. Hell, for that matter, he could dust his cactus and maybe check the mailbox, not that there was ever much of anything in it.

He hated it when conspiracies brewed around him. But he drove across the square, parked at the jail and got out, morosely glancing over his shoulder at the Tulips Saloon.

Just then he saw the biggest traitor of them all sneak through the stained-glass doors like a garden snake into a watering can—Zach. His own brother!

No doubt Liberty was in there. Of course she was. She would be right in the thick of the action, surrounded by her friends.

He felt the urge to cross the street and crash the party, feigning that his invitation had been misplaced. Maybe it had been? But his sister would have dragged him in, at least, if she'd thought he'd been invited, which meant he most definitely had not.

And he'd vowed to stay clear of Liberty, to give her a taste of her own medicine.

"Damn it," he muttered. His heart was breaking. To be ousted from the town he loved, snubbed by people he spent his days helping…

What had gone so wrong between he and Liberty? One second he'd had her at the altar, the next, she'd disappeared. He should be angry, but all he did was love her more. Her wild side appealed to him.

And damn it, that's exactly what he was going to tell her. He was going to walk into the Tulips Saloon like the sheriff he was—this time he'd even gently ease open the doors instead of tossing them back—and he'd politely ask for his dog. That's what he'd do.

It wouldn't work, he realized, because Mr. Parsons was in there and she probably wouldn't even leave the old man's side.

Okay, so he'd cruise over there and just act as if he hadn't known there was a party. It wasn't Ladies Only Day so he had every right, he assured himself righteously while taking a swig of whiskey in some cold coffee for courage.

Gathering up his bravado, which had been shamelessly stomped lately, he strode across the street. With good manners and a somewhat trembling heart, he calmly opened the doors with a smile that he hoped would convey *I'm harmless, aren't we friends?*

Silence enveloped the room. The smile slipped from his face as he saw the rangy cowboy sitting next to Liberty. Hesitating—remembering to keep a lid on his temper—his gaze suddenly riveted to the beautiful cake Liberty was about to cut.

The cake was festooned with a tier of pastel pink-and-blue ribbons, and a silver baby rattle lay beneath it like a shiny announcement of a beautiful, miraculous future.

His eyes met Liberty's with horror and heartbreak, and in her eyes he read the truth: Liberty Wentworth was welcoming a baby into her life. That was the real reason she'd returned to Tulips.

What a faithless would-be-bride she'd turned out to be.

Chapter Four

"Duke, wait!" Liberty hurried after him as he strode down the street. Catching his arm, she made him stop so that she could catch her breath. Duke snatched his arm away from her grasp and her heart broke, even more than it had when he'd peeked around the saloon door, his face hopeful and trusting. "Please let me explain."

"There's nothing to explain." He headed for the jailhouse—his sanctuary—but she followed relentlessly.

"If you would just wait a minute, Duke," she said.

"Obviously, I've been waiting too long."

There was a stitch in her side but she followed him into his office before he could somehow lock her out. She didn't want to cause more of a scene than they already had, and she knew too well that a few dozen faces were tucked up against the windows of the Tulips Saloon, anxiously peering out. "Duke, can I just explain?"

He turned on her. "Explain that you're pregnant?" he demanded, his harsh voice tearing in her heart. She'd never seen his eyes so cold. "I don't think that requires an explanation, Liberty. And I do think I now understand why I wasn't invited to the shower."

"It wasn't really a shower." It had turned into one, but quite by accident, though she doubted he was in the mood to hear that.

"So, everyone knew but me." He looked at her, shaking his head in disbelief. "And I guess wearing the wedding gown the other day means you're marrying that pup who was paying court at your feet."

She was astonished he would think such a thing. "Duke, that cowboy came with Valentine to help her deliver the cake. I didn't know that Pansy and Helen had ordered one." She put a hand on his arm. "Please hear me out. This has all gotten way out of hand."

"I don't want to listen," Duke said, and Liberty recognized the strong Duke, the one with all the stubborn opinions, marching in to stiffen his spine and his resolve. There'd be no talking to him now.

"Just go on," he told Liberty. "I can't take any more drama. Honestly. In fact, I think I'll let all of you schemers have my sheriff's seat. I've got a hankering to live in the tropics around some beautiful beauties who just want to feed me pineapples all day."

Liberty blinked. Now was not the time to tell him, she realized with a pang. As mad as he was now, the truth would fall on dry, hard soil.

"But congratulations. I guess," he said.

She sat on his desk. "You're going to have to listen."

"Ah. A prisoner in my own jail. I don't think I do have to listen." He reclined in the old cracked leather chair, putting his boots up on the desk and covering his face with his hat.

"Duke," Liberty said, irritated, "this isn't easy for me."

He was silent.

"Must you be a troll?"

She thought she heard snoring.

She *did* hear snoring. His chest fell with rhythmic breathing, and she knew he really had nodded off, just like that, out of sheer determination to shut her out. "You're the daddy," she said softly, just to try out the words.

Not a hitch in those z's. Rip Van Winkle wasn't about to be disturbed by some climactic pronouncement.

She wanted to cry but all of her tears had been squeezed out of her long ago. Being strong didn't mean a woman couldn't cry, but it did mean she usually had better things to do with her time, so Liberty left Duke in his state of slumber and departed.

It was very still across the street, as if the Tulips Saloon was waiting for life to be breathed back into it. Liberty straightened her shoulders and walked through the pretty, stained-glass doors.

All her friends sat at tables, waiting to see whether she would need comforting or if wedding bells would finally ring. Sadness and a bit of embarrassment clutched at her. "I'm sorry," she said. "I couldn't tell him."

He wouldn't listen was more the truth, but it didn't seem fair to air every piece of their dirty laundry.

Pansy opened her arms, and Liberty rushed into them, squeezing her eyes tightly shut so that she wouldn't see Duke's face, so crestfallen when he realized his own town had left him out-and it was all because of Liberty.

"YOU COULDN'T HAVE BEEN more of a pissant if you'd tried, Duke," Pepper said to her older brother late that afternoon when he slunk home, tired despite his nap. Duke glanced at her, then at Zach, with some surprise. Pepper was lying out in a bikini around the pool, soaking up some waning September sunshine after being up north so long, and Zach was coiling up a hose he'd been using to water the plants around the patio.

"Just let it drop," Duke commanded, unwilling to talk to anyone about what had happened. He had no idea what his brother's and sister's roles had been in today's drama, but what he did know was that they, and most of the town, were on Liberty's side.

Damned if he knew why.

Zach shrugged, not about to throw any weight on his side of the sinking ship to save him, Duke realized. There would be no peace in his house until they'd had their say, obviously. "Spit out all the opinions you want, and then the matter's closed," he stated, feeling angry that his own siblings were against him. Who could you count on if not family?

With a sigh, Pepper went back to reading a magazine. It was a medical journal, Duke saw as she defiantly flipped pages. Zach went inside, abandoning the whole family council process.

Though Duke should have felt relief, the silent treatment just brought him more anxiety. Shouldn't someone recognize that he wasn't the enemy?

Of course, it wasn't often that Pepper was put out with him. For as long as he could remember, he and his siblings had been tight as ticks.

Liberty had been the one knot in the tight rope of their existence. As a child, she'd sneaked across the small ravine, deftly climbing the barbed-wire fence of their property and playing pranks on them. It had been like having their own personal, mischief-making elf. Milk would disappear. Pots would be rearranged on the patio. A cow would be wearing a bow around its neck at Christmas. Once she'd put firecrackers in their mailbox. Small ones, of course, but it had gotten their attention.

And then they'd laid a trap for her, figuring to put a stop to the antics of the Wentworth waif. One Christmas Eve night, they put candy canes all along the patio leading to the front door, a colorful sugar trail designed to catch a child who was doubling their chores with her mischief. As they sat at the family Christmas table, laden with home-cooked food and covered with fine linen, they innocently waited to see if they'd have a visitor.

When they heard the cowbell clang and the bucket release its four gallons of water, they knew they had her and went gleefully dashing from the table.

Liberty had been standing on the porch, soaking wet, caught in the act of staring in the window at them before taking off at a run. Their mother, coming up behind them, had seen the two handprints she'd left against the window as she'd peered in, and it wasn't Liberty who got in trouble that night. Their father had given Duke, Zach and Pepper such a talking to, and then their mother had marched them over to the Wentworths to apologize to Liberty and her parents.

What they'd seen in the Wentworth home had surprised them. There was no Christmas table adorned with glowing candles and laden with home-cooked food. No decorations. Mr. and Mrs. Wentworth sat in front of a fire, each reading a book, completely unaware that their daughter had been gone at all, and apparently disinterested that it was Christmas Eve.

But what Duke never forgot was the look in Liberty's eyes as she stared at his mother—it was the hungry look of a child who desperately wanted the attention his mother was giving her. His mother toweled off Liberty and then handed her the strand of candy canes they'd used as bait. Not only that, she went back and retrieved the presents he and his siblings were supposed to get for Christmas that year and gave them to Liberty.

He'd resented that, until he saw those three toys in Mr. Parsons's pawnshop window and realized Liberty had never even gotten to play with them.

From that day forward, she was one of them. She ate at their table for meals, and she walked to school with them. Zach was her same age so they became the closest, though Pepper had followed Liberty around like fog.

He had tried to hold himself aloof, as he'd been uncertain of her. Thirteen years old, he'd been a jumble of hormones and teenage pride and not sure what to think about the little girl who, once she was cleaned up, stoked some part of his being he hadn't been aware existed. Oh, the girls chased him, and he ignored them for the most part, because he'd been interested in football and baseball and rodeo.

But Liberty nagged at him, and he was never quite sure what to do with those confusing feelings. So he ignored her.

But one time he'd come upon her and Zach and Holt in the barn attic, and he was astonished by what he saw. Liberty and Zach had dressed Holt in a costume, an old wrangler's outfit for Halloween, and they were busily sewing and stuffing material on him. Holt was the sewing dummy, or whatever one called those things, and they were improvising.

Duke couldn't even thread a needle, wouldn't have known how to start, and the jealousy that hit him took him clean by surprise. When Zach wore the costume to the Halloween Ball in town that night, Duke had been positively pea-green.

And he really hadn't understood why. As costumes went, they all looked fine. Liberty was a bride, Pepper was a witch—not too far off the mark there, he'd thought with brotherly snideness—and Holt, who tagged along, was a British punk rocker. Duke wore his football uniform with streaks of grease under his eyes, in no way feeling dressed up at all.

When Zach won "Best Costume" that night, Liberty hugged him with glee and kissed Holt's cheek, and Duke knew something special had happened he'd been left out of: Liberty's secret mission.

She was going to design things. And he would be left out, because he had no patience for thread and small stitches and lace, and wouldn't stand still and be a sewing mannequin.

But Zach and Holt would.

"So are you going to sit there and sigh all day, or are you going to say what's on your mind?" Duke demanded. "I can tell you're about to burst with advice."

"No," Pepper said, giving him a bland look over her journal. "I'm not."

"Oh, come on," Duke said. "You need to give me the blah-blah-blah so you'll feel you've done your part to demoralize big bro. Pardon me—I meant, shove common sense into big bro's lumpy thick skull. Sermonize is the word I'm looking for."

Pepper laughed. "Don't be a pissant with me, Duke. I don't have to take it like poor Liberty does."

Poor Liberty didn't take anything from anybody. "Liberty does what Liberty likes." And that included stranding him at the altar in a dress she'd designed just for the occasion. No doubt she would now be wearing maternity clothes she'd designed as well.

He'd never forgive her.

He went inside, feeling a shower might ease the knot of tension at the base of his skull. The knot in his heart couldn't be eased at all.

"I think Pepper's right," Zach hollered from the kitchen. "As much as I hate to gang up on you. You need to nail your boots to the floor, if that's what it takes, and be still and silent until Liberty's gotten to say everything she needs to."

Duke went in to face his brother. "When did you learn about the party today? Excuse me for thinking you're a traitor, but somehow I have this feeling you should have mentioned that my ex-fiancée was having a baby shower."

Zach mashed his hat down low on his head and drummed his fingers on the chopping block before setting down the knife he'd been cutting onions with. "I didn't know until Pepper told me. And Pepper didn't know until Pansy called her. No one really knew until the last minute. Pansy accidentally read some notes she'd written wrong. The macular degeneration makes it hard for her to see some pieces of letters sometimes, and she got the date mixed up. Today was the day Valentine was bringing out a couple of cakes for Helen to choose from, only Pansy misread and called around to ask a few people if they knew today was the day, and we all scrambled to get there. It was entirely a miscommunication. Although it did turn out nice," he said happily, munching a bell pepper. "I do love anything Valentine bakes."

"Which does mean that everyone in fact knew of a baby shower, which means everyone knew that Liberty was pregnant." He glared at his brother. "Except me."

"You're not on the grapevine, that's for sure," Zach agreed. "Gossip doesn't exactly flow through your office. Does your phone even work? Mr. Parsons hasn't been picking up lately."

Shouldn't the sheriff know as much or more than any of his citizens? He relished his role of plot-buster. How had the ladies gotten two plots past him in one week? And what else was bubbling in their cauldron? "Why doesn't gossip flow through my office?"

"Because you take yourself so seriously," Zach said, "and frankly, no one in their right mind was going to tell you that Liberty was pregnant. That wouldn't be gossiping. That would be…" His words trailed off under Duke's withering stare.

"Would be?"

"Dangerous," Zach said. "Where you got your hot temper from, I'll never know. Dad didn't have much of one. Mom sure wasn't hot-tempered. But where Liberty's concerned, you're an eager spark. I sure hope you don't pass that temper of yours on to your—"

Zach froze, his eyes wide.

Duke's antennae went straight up, quivering. "Go on," he said silkily. "You were saying something about passing my temper?"

Zach hurriedly chopped peppers and onions and then part of his hand. "Damn!" he exclaimed, sucking on his finger for drama, Duke was certain, because there was no blood. "Go away, Duke. You've completely destroyed my focus!"

Duke grunted and left, annoyed with both his siblings. He sat on the porch, leaned against a pillar and stared up at the late-evening sky, feeling a lot like Mr. Carmine searching the heavens for something meaningful and finding goose formations to admire instead. It felt as if the world was against him. His dog had deserted him. His fiancée was more than just an ex; she was enlarging her world with a baby and leaving him behind again, in a matter of speaking. His citizens—and they were his—were plotting against him, and his office. Everything that mattered to him was leaving him in a desperate state of helplessness, which he hated, but the thing he hated most was that Liberty didn't love him anymore.

And all he wanted to do was kiss her lips and hear her sigh his name.

It just wasn't fair to want something as much as he wanted her. But she just wasn't going to say, "Yes, Duke," like he wished she would.

Maybe if she were more easygoing, everything would have worked out. Still, something nagged at him.

Something that said maybe, just maybe, his sheriff's hat had gotten a bit tight on his big, stubborn head. It occurred to him that maybe pride was a meal worth swallowing when his dessert could be eating wedding cake from the fingers of his beautiful bride.

Chapter Five

"It's not working," Pansy said to Helen as they sat at a table with Valentine and Liberty the next morning. Floral teacups and delicate bowls filled with fruit covered a lace tablecloth, but despite the festive decorations the mood of the women in the room was somber. "This whole Ladies Only Day appears to have gone awry."

Liberty looked at Valentine. "Tulips will be a harder town to build than Union Junction, most likely."

Valentine shook her head. "Men will be drawn to your eligible bachelorettes. It's just that the whole concept is in its early stages. And remember, mine was a Men's Day, designed to flatter the local menfolk for Father's Day."

"What Pansy means," Helen said with authority, "was that we can't even get the eligible bachelors and bachelorettes we have in this town on the same pony, much less bring men to this town for some of our beautiful girls."

Liberty shook her head. "I agree with Valentine. We've only just begun to build the town, and the concept is somewhat transparent. We've made the day about our social time, when we should have made it about our talent and our attributes. And that Tulips is the perfect place for growing families." Liberty was quiet for a moment, then said, "We need to hold a ball."

Valentine stared at her. Pansy and Helen sat up straight.

"And invite men from nearby towns who are interested in finding a wife," Liberty said. "Not me, of course, but the women here who would love a man to date."

"Why not you?" Valentine asked.

"Not me because…I don't dance," she said instead of saying *because I have loved Duke all my life even though he's a stubborn ape.* "But I design very beautiful gowns," she said, "and I have lots of beautiful things to dress up our town's fair ladies in."

Pansy blinked. "What about Duke?"

"What about him?"

"Well, someone would have to tell him our

plan," Helen said, "and so far as I can tell, he hasn't been in a receptive mood. He doesn't have much patience with this whole Ladies Only Day idea, and when we tell him we're expanding it—"

"Tweaking it," Valentine said. "It would become a Tulips Day, like Union Junction's Men's Day."

"It's still not working," Helen said. "Your day was to celebrate your men. Our day would be to showcase our debs, spinsters and widows."

"And I don't want to give up our Ladies Only Day," Pansy said. "I look forward to our monthly meetings."

"We talk every day," Helen said.

Pansy added, "I know. It drives Duke mad."

Liberty leaned forward. "But he'd like it if we called it Tulips Men's Day. We could tell him we were turning over a new leaf and making it all about men."

They took that in for a moment. Pansy's gray eyebrows furrowed. Helen's little mouth bowed. Valentine picked at the fruit bowl in front of her, lining up the strawberries and blueberries in a decorative row.

"It's good," Valentine finally said. "It's exactly the kind of thing we would have done to get around the Jefferson brothers of Malfunction Junction. Appeal to their machismo and manly pride."

"Actually," Pansy said slowly, "we're just really talking around the one thing that we've messed up, which is all my fault. Liberty, I'm so sorry that I got Duke upset with you. Even more upset than he already is. Er, was."

"Is and was," Liberty said, "and Duke's been in a perpetual state of irritation with me ever since he discovered I had returned to Tulips. Don't blame yourself at all," she told her friend, hugging Pansy to her and feeling the frailness of her bones and the softness of her hair. "Besides, how could I be mad at you? You ladies are my dearest friends."

"Excuse me," Duke said, his sudden appearance startling all of them. His gaze bounced to Liberty and then away. "Have any of you seen my dog?"

Helen shook her head. "She's not here."

"She's not with Mr. Parsons, either." Duke frowned and Liberty could see the concern on his face. "Mr. Parsons says he thought she went off with that young cowboy who was here." He glared at Liberty.

"Blaine?" Valentine smiled at Duke. "Blaine went down to the Chop House to get a burger. I believe I did see a flash of gold slinking after him, now that I think about it."

"Oh."

Duke appeared to be unsatisfied with that information. Liberty smiled at him to try to make him relax, but the old magic didn't work on him. He glared at her again, said, "Thanks, ladies," and left.

Helen sighed. "It's going to be very ugly around here for a while. I think the best thing we could all do is steer clear of the sheriff until his mood improves."

Liberty felt Pansy squeeze her hand and hug her a little more, and it did help—some. But not as much as it would have if Duke had given her a bit of a glance that didn't have ice on it.

DUKE WENT BACK to his office, not about to run after his faithless dog. But to have Molly go off with Liberty's new cowboy friend was just too much!

"That was fast," Mr. Parsons said, glancing up from straightening his cell when Duke strode into his office and threw himself into his desk chair. "Did you find her?"

"Our dog has gone off with a strange man," Duke said. "Something we should have told her is unacceptable."

"I meant Liberty," Mr. Parsons said, and Duke sighed.

"Liberty is where she always is, tightly knit into the town beehive with the queen bees who are after my hide."

"Think there's only one queen per hive," Mr. Parsons said, but Duke was too miserable to care. His dog, his woman, his town—they were all slipping from his grasp. He watched Mr. Parsons pick objects up from a shelf, expertly dust under them and then replace them. Carefully, the elderly man tucked a small ledger book into a copper box, making certain it was locked.

"What's that, Mr. Parsons?" Duke asked.

"The town records." Mr. Parsons patted the old box with satisfaction. "All the private information is right here in my safekeeping, safe from bees and every other type of varmint." He grinned at Duke, but Duke was looking around his office.

"Shouldn't the town records be in there?" He pointed to the only filing cabinet in the room, which he knew for certain held property deeds, auto deeds and anything else a registrar's office would contain.

"This is how Mrs. Gaines kept them for thirty years," Mr. Parsons said, "and after she died, and I took over the position, I really saw no reason to move them into that." He jerked his head toward the three-drawer filing cabinet. "Seems like important stuff would be easy for anyone to get into if it were in that thing. I don't really trust it."

Duke blinked. "How is that copper box safer?"

"No one cares about this old box. Besides, no one comes in my bedroom."

That was true. Still, Duke felt that something was amiss. "You're not actually...the registrar," he said slowly. "Nor are you a town official—you used to own the town pawnshop. Should you be in possession of private documents?"

"Who are they safer with?" Mr. Parsons looked at him with sympathy. "After the ladies vote Zach into office, along with Pepper, you'll not have any business in here, anyway. It's best if there's a firm, ongoing, permanent hand on our town records."

Duke slid back into his chair, thinking, even as he dismissed Mr. Parsons's assertion, that the ladies were conspiring against him. He could deal with that later. "Does anybody know you have the box?"

"You. You're the sheriff, and you're all that matters in that regard. For the moment you're the sheriff, anyway."

Duke ignored that rumination. "Do you ever look inside it?"

Mr. Parsons nodded. "Of course I do. When

Sheriff Widow Gaines died, I counted every single document to make certain they were all there. She told me exactly how she liked them kept when I visited her in the hospital, and I've done it exactly the way she felt was best."

Duke frowned. "But wouldn't that make those public records then? Not to put too fine a point on it, but that's sort of how it's looking to me."

"No," Mr. Parsons said, "these are not tax nor property records. These are birth certificates, medical examiner certificates, marriage certificates—"

"In other words, there's not a whole lot in that damn box," Duke said. There weren't very many people in the town, and the last citizen of Tulips who'd passed on was Mrs. Gaines, rest her soul.

"Nope. Not until the new little settler is born."

"Settler?" Duke's frown deepened. What else didn't he know about?

"Liberty's baby," Mr. Parsons said mildly, "our first town birth in years."

"Give me a peek at the box," Duke said.

"Hell, no, Sheriff," Mr. Parsons said. "You should never open up a box. Nothing good ever came of opening up a box that your eyes weren't meant to see into. Think of Pandora, for example."

Duke wondered if any other sheriff in the history of the planet had as little power as he did. The truth was, he didn't do a damn thing except respond to disturbance-of-the-peace calls, and those were usually between the women and the few men of the town when they somehow got crosswise with each other. Other than that, the ladies did what they pleased, and the men had their own code of survival.

He wasn't even in charge of the town secrets. Heaven only knew, there couldn't be many. He'd known these people all their lives. "I'm bored," he said, suddenly realizing it was true.

"Well, getting into this box isn't going to help. Go play Monopoly," Mr. Parsons shot back. "Get one of those fancy computers. Learn to program in your spare time."

"Program what?"

"How about something to spy on the woman," Mr. Parsons whispered dramatically. "They've got their own spying methods, you know."

Duke grunted. "I believe that's illegal."

Molly-Jimbo ran in the door with a great doggie smile on her face, fresh from eating a burger. He could tell she had because she was waving her plumy tail, and the wonderfully smoky smell of the grill wafted over to him as she ran straight into Mr. Parsons's cell.

"Just great," Duke said.

The cowboy—Blaine—poked his head inside Duke's office, nodding at him and Mr. Parsons. "Just making sure this is where your dog belonged, sir."

"That's fine. Thank you," Duke said, squashing the urge to go smash some baby-shower cake. "Don't get hit crossing the street," he muttered after the cowboy had left.

"That wasn't nice," Mr. Parsons said.

Duke sighed. No, it wasn't. Now he was getting graded on his manners. His marks were bad, and frankly, he realized he needed a change. "Back to my boredom problem," he said, but Mr. Parsons closed his cell door with a clang.

Duke blinked. Of course, one could see right through the bars, so it wasn't as if he were completely shut out. It wasn't the same as slamming a wooden door, but Duke got the hint.

"You're not bored, you're mad," Mr. Parsons said, "and my suggestion to you is that you go get your problems with your woman straightened out and quit avoiding them like every other man in this town does. Now, Jimbo and I are going to take a nap."

It was probably the best advice he'd heard yet. "Well, I guess I'll go stick my head in the beehive. I can't get any more stung than I've already been."

Mr. Parsons didn't reply so Duke went out into the fresh night air, wondering if he'd be better off heading down to the Chop House himself. Everyone thought he was the bad guy, which wasn't fair, because he was the one who'd gotten left at the altar.

But Liberty was the only woman he was ever going to love. He wondered how he could feel this way when he knew she was pregnant by another man. If she thought he was going to fight that young pup Blaine for her—what a silly name— she was sadly mistaken. Either she loved him, or she loved that young child who probably hadn't shaved more than ten summers, but Duke wasn't going to beg for her love. No, sir.

And there she was, coming out of the saloon with an armful of presents, walking toward the center of town. Because he was a gentleman—and not because he was looking for an excuse—he hurried after her.

Before he'd even reached her, Liberty said, "I can carry them," and tried to avoid his reach.

Duke grabbed a stuffed monkey, a music box and a basket full of baby wipes and diapers before she could protest further. "We could put all this in my truck and make one trip of it," he said, "especially for that white wicker baby pram."

Liberty stopped and glared at him. "How do you know about the pram?"

"I saw Valentine pushing it inside the saloon."

"Why didn't you stay if you knew about the party?"

"Because I wasn't invited."

"No one was invited, Duke," Liberty said impatiently. "If anybody would have been invited properly, if Pansy hadn't made an innocent little error, believe me, you would have been the *first* to get an invitation."

"I would have?" He suddenly felt better.

"Yes," Liberty said, her tone still curt.

"Why do I not feel like that's a good thing?" he asked, wondering which of his many transgressions she was annoyed with at this moment.

She turned down a small street and walked up on the porch of a small white gingerbread house, which, it turned out, was next to Helen's yellow-painted house and Pansy's redbrick house. She let herself in, and Duke stopped on the wooden porch.

"I thought you were staying with Pansy or Helen," he said.

"I bought a house. This house." Liberty smiled as she set down the presents on a table. "It's all mine. The first thing I've ever completely owned."

His stomach did a funny churn. In his mind, Liberty still lived in the house at the back of his ranch, even though her parents had sold it years ago and moved away to a commune somewhere. A real estate developer had bought it, and no one had lived in the house since. "I can't see myself living here," he murmured.

"You don't live here," she said, surprised. "I mean, why would you see yourself living here?"

He looked at her. "I don't know. It's such a doll's house." In fact, it was so dainty he couldn't see anyone but Liberty living there. A feeling of panic set in, a sensation that he was completely out of touch with every inhabitant in Tulips and possibly every person he'd ever known in his entire life. What the hell was he supposed to say to the woman he loved when she became a home-owner? "Why didn't my office receive the deed?" he asked stupidly. "Shouldn't I have received some tax notification or something?"

Liberty looked at him. "Duke, this is not your kingdom and you do not sit on a throne. Not everything that happens in Tulips is going to be notified through the sheriff's office." She turned away from him, giving him a view of a stiffly straight back and a delicious nape, which, as matters were going, he might not ever get to kiss again. "My loan went through Holt," she said.

"Holt? Our town hairdresser?" Duke shook his head. "He can't give you a loan."

"He sold me this house, which was one of six he owns in this town," Liberty said defensively.

How had that information slipped past him? "Well, congratulations are in order, Liberty. I'm… happy for you." He wasn't, not really, because he knew this place wasn't meant for a big man like him to live in, and that Liberty hadn't considered that when purchasing it. But that meant she also wasn't planning on the pup, the Blaine character, who seemed to be trying to write himself into the play that was Liberty's life.

"Duke, we need to talk," Liberty said.

He glanced around at the still-unpacked boxes. Maybe it wasn't too late to change her mind about this fragile house. "I'm listening."

"You're *not* listening," she said, which caught him off guard because it was true, so he tried to focus more on the moment and less on matters he couldn't change.

She took a deep breath. "This is hard for me to tell you. Very hard. But this baby—" Hesitating, she put a hand on her stomach for a second. "This is our child. *We're* having a baby."

Chapter Six

Duke went pale, and Liberty's heart tightened. She couldn't breathe. He wasn't happy, that much was clear. There was shock mixed with denial, and maybe anger, on his face. "Oh, Duke," she murmured. "I am so sorry."

They stared at each other for a long moment. His mouth worked as though he wanted to speak but couldn't. Then it looked as if his legs were giving out as he sat down on the old sofa and stared at her.

Liberty had tried many times to envision Duke's reaction to her news, had given herself every chance to prepare for several scenarios of his possible emotions. But she hadn't imagined this stunned silence. "Duke—" she began.

He surged to his feet. "Marry me. Right now. Say yes, and this time, damn it, stay at the altar."

She drew in a breath. "Duke—"

He picked up the stuffed monkey he'd carried into the house, stared at it for a second, then tossed it back down. "Liberty, every single person in this town knows I'm the father, don't they?"

"Since I've never cared for anyone but you, they probably guessed," Liberty responded.

He thought about Mr. Parsons's copper box. "By heaven, and took bets on it, too," he said.

"Sure, they bet on everything. Why are you so surprised?"

He pushed back his hat. "It's illegal, for one thing, but never mind that. Did you know that they've taken up spying?"

"Well, it's more ham radio operating and things of that nature," she said. "I wouldn't call it international espionage just yet."

"How do you know all this? Why don't I?" Shaking his head, he said, "I'm not getting sidetracked. The very fact that I didn't know any of this is the problem. Everybody knows everything, including the fact that you're expecting my child, and I appear to be the one person in this town everyone leaves in the dark!"

"You stay holed up in your office most of the time. How could you expect to know more than you do?" Liberty asked.

"I expect to know when I become a father!" Crossing to her, he took her hand. "Liberty Wentworth, this time you're going to marry me. I asked you nicely and romantically the first time but it didn't get me past the altar, and so this time, I'm telling you, you're staying at the altar if I have to glue your little white shoes to the floor!"

"I think you're in shock, and I think you and I both need to think things through rationally. Neither of us wants to make a mistake in judgment," Liberty said, pulling her hand away, but Duke continued to hold her up close to him.

"I know you don't. And I know why. But you're not on the outside looking in anymore, Liberty. You belong to this town, and you belong to me. You're having my baby, and I care about that, and I care about you." He let her go, his fingers leaving sweetly warm places on her skin. "The wedding carousel ends right here. This time, you're going to face all your fears and see my wedding ring on your finger. Where it will remain. Forever."

Her heart began a dangerous palpitation, spilling nervous tension throughout her body. She wanted him to stop talking! His gaze wouldn't release her, though he didn't touch her again. Still, she stood, rooted by his words.

It was true, every word he'd said. She *was* afraid, terribly afraid. And he wasn't making her feel any better. "Duke, the reason I didn't go through with it in the first place is that I knew we weren't right for each other." She tried to carefully choose her words so they'd at least end up friends, which at the moment seemed like a distant dream. "You're too bullheaded for me. And for most everyone else in this town. We don't mean to avoid you or leave you out, but we know your opinions and your personality will far dominate the decisions we're trying to make at that moment. You're more of a parent than a friend. That image summarizes the situation as best I can."

"I'm going to be a parent now!"

"Town father. That's what you are." Liberty turned away, not able to face the hurt expression Duke wore. "You make an excellent sheriff for that very reason."

"Which is why the little blue-haired women are trying to take my job and put Pepper and Zach in it," he stated roughly.

"Oh, don't call them that," Liberty said. "Holt mixes beautiful shades of gray."

He sighed. "I'm using an outdated expression, and I apologize, and for the name-calling—however endearingly I mean it. It's all outdated."

She turned to him. "You are a trifle outdated, you know. You want to rule, possess, own, conquer."

"What's wrong with that?" His chin jutted out.

"Maybe nothing—to some other woman out there, Duke," she said, her voice soft.

"But I had to find the one hell-raising woman to get pregnant." He sighed. "Things just never come easy for me somehow."

Liberty tapped his arm. "You're hardheaded, Duke. Even you admit it."

He looked at her. "Liberty, you liked me well enough to go to bed with me. Now you're going to have to deal with me, hardheaded, annoying, opinionated and every other tag you and my townspeople need to describe me. But deal with me you will. And marry me you will."

He walked out, leaving her stunned at his abrupt departure. Then she realized she hadn't heard his boots leave her porch. Waiting, she held her breath.

As she'd expected, he poked his head around the door.

"By the way, I suppose I should say congratulations," he said begrudgingly.

"To you as well," she replied cautiously.

"You're a…beautiful mother."

She realized he was trying to make an effort at chivalry, as foreign as it was to his tongue. "Thank you."

He glanced around the room, then back at her with as much suspicion as he might view a snake. "I assume we're not due for a while yet?"

"I'm seven months pregnant," she said.

His face went completely ashen. "You can't be! I can't even tell you're pregnant."

"If I took off my clothes, you certainly would. Besides, my figure seems to camouflage it well. It's my height. At least that's what Pansy said."

He blinked. "But you were just trying on your wedding gown the other day."

"Trying is the operative verb. We couldn't get it fastened, not really. Without the Cinderella styling, the dress would never have even gotten that close."

"Seven months," he murmured. "That means two to go until we have a…baby."

"I can't marry you, Duke," she said softly. "Please don't make this harder on me than it is. I came home because I didn't want to keep your child from you. But I really don't want this to be an uncomfortable thing between us."

"It's too late for that." He gave her one last hard look, then let the door close.

This time she heard his boots clomp away. Then silence enveloped her.

For the first time, she fully understood how he'd felt when she'd walked away from him at the altar.

"WELL, WE SURE AS HELL can't give him a bachelor party," Mr. Parsons said to Pansy and Helen and Bug Carmine.

"And I don't think a baby shower is what he wants, either. He seemed pretty sore that we accidentally gave Liberty one before he knew about the baby."

"Duke's sore about everything these days," Helen said, not caring much about that. The sheriff was just going to have to get himself sorted out. The main thing on her mind was Liberty and the coming baby. "Let's just focus on how we take care of Liberty, and then what we want to do about growing the town. We ladies have voted on a Men's Day. What have you men come up with?"

The four of them sat in the front room of Pansy's house, and from her large picture window they had an excellent view of anything of interest that went on outside. They'd seen Duke stomp off, for example, and knew he and Liberty weren't exactly falling in love like a couple of teenagers.

"We've not come up with a damn thing," Bug

said. "And we're not sure Duke's going to rubber-stamp the Men's Day thing. The last thing on his mind will be growing the town. He's got his own 'growth' on his mind."

"He'll definitely be too overwhelmed now," Mr. Parsons said. "Liberty's got him in a twist."

"It's his own fault," Pansy said crossly, and they all stared at her, shocked because she was never out of sorts. "He's such a *man*."

"Oh, no," Bug said, "let's don't drag out Man-Cussin' 101."

"Pooh," Helen said. "You keep running off like you do, Bug, and one of these days, your wife's gonna give you the goodbye boot, right in your saggy—"

"We're all setting a bad example for Duke and Liberty, and all our young people," Pansy interrupted, her voice quavering. "It's not like any of us really get along with each other. We really just form partnerships out of necessity. And how is that inspirational?"

They thought about that for a minute, and Helen almost wished Pansy hadn't pointed out the truth. Pansy didn't mean she and Helen didn't get along, of course, but it was true that "The Battle Of The Sexes" raged fiercely in Tulips.

In the nicest kind of way, of course.

"Who is the real villain here?" she asked. "Why can't we get anything right?"

"Well, the villain is not a sole thing or person," Mr. Parsons said importantly. "It's many persons and things."

"Such as?" Helen demanded.

He looked at them all. "My name's Hiram. Don't think I've ever heard any of you call me that in the entire time I've been living here."

Pansy's eyes bugged. "You're too old for any of us to refer to you by your first name, you old goat! That doesn't make us villains, it makes us mindful of our manners and good upbreeding!"

Bug snickered. Helen stared at Pansy.

"You're no spring chicken," Hiram Parsons said with some dignity, "and my point is that we never get past the surface niceties with one another. The formal veneer, if you will."

"What does that have to do with Duke and Liberty? Or even a villain in the piece?" Pansy asked. "I'm going to need some more tea if you keep this nonsense up, *Hiram*."

The handsome elderly gentleman shrugged. "To understand what we need to do, we have to dig deeper."

Helen blinked. "If we dig any deeper, Duke's going to tell us to mind our own business."

Bug nodded. "No one likes their skeletons dragged out in the open for public scrutiny."

They stared at him for a minute.

"What if I told you," Hiram said, lowering his voice for an instant, though no one could hear them outside the cozy kitchen, "that every single person at this table is hiding a secret? And that each of our secrets could, in fact, change Tulips and the way it operates, forever?"

Helen's heart began a slow pound. "If we did, why would it matter?"

Now everyone looked at her curiously. Helen felt a hot flush creep up her neck.

"Because *we're* the villains," Hiram said. "We're just as guilty as anyone else of being prideful and stubborn and deceitful. So why do we try to fit, say, Liberty and Duke, into a tidy, perfect box?" He blinked at them. "We certainly couldn't live up to that kind of close inspection."

"You're right," Bug said. "We're like overeager parents trying to do everything for our children because we want to protect them from stumbling and falling."

Pansy looked at them owlishly behind her glasses. "I think you're trying to get out of having a ball, Hiram Parsons."

He waved his hand. "I'm only pointing out that

maybe Tulips is what Tulips is, and all this striving to make it better might actually make it worse. Maybe we should just leave well enough alone and let the town grow naturally."

"Heaven forbid we should get up off our lazy hides and bones to improve ourselves," Helen said tartly. "If that's your idea of villainy, it's dumb."

A knock sounded on the door, making them all jump. "It's Duke," Helen said, "I can see his hat through the glass."

"Poor Duke," Pansy said, getting up to let him in. "Surrounded by villains. Helen, put the kettle on to boil, please. I'm sure the man could use a good hot steaming cup of fortifying tea before he faces the town baddies."

Helen noted Bug and Hiram sat up straighter and smiled at hearing "put the kettle on to boil." More tea meant more cookies—the big babies, Helen thought. No villains at this table, unless cookie-begging could be considered a crime.

Duke followed Pansy inside and took the hat off his head out of politeness—but didn't wipe the scowl from his face.

"I've got something to say," he said, and they all looked at him expectantly.

"Every one of you in this room knew Liberty was expecting my child, and not one of you told me." He looked at each of them individually, giving everyone a very narrow, disappointed gaze. Helen felt herself shrink a bit inside her starched dress.

"Congratulations, Duke," Pansy offered.

"Well, I should say thank you, and I might even be happy, except that none of my friends cared to give me the good news."

"We felt it was Liberty's place," Bug offered. "We're not much for poking our noses into other people's business."

Duke grunted. "I disagree. The town's resident schemers sit at this table, and you two," he said to Pansy and Helen, "are the very worst."

Pansy gasped. Helen patted her friend's hand. Darn Duke for being such a blunt speaker!

"The plotting stops today," he said firmly. "Right now. No more keeping things from me. No more hiding, secreting and ferreting away from me. We've had our fun with the game of 'what the sheriff doesn't know won't hurt us,' but now you've gone too far. And I blame you two the most."

"Blame yourself," Helen said. "We weren't the ones engaging in premarital affection."

The room went silent.

"Without birth control, even," Pansy piped in, moving the moment from minor embarrassment to downright too-much-information. "You can't pin this situation on us, Duke."

Duke glared at her. "A man has a right to know that he's a father!"

"But we didn't have the right to tell you," Mr. Parsons pointed out. "As you know, Duke, I pride myself on my ability to keep my silence on the private matters of people living in Tulips."

Duke stared at the four people sitting at the table with some consternation. What they were saying was true. He couldn't blame them for keeping quiet about Liberty's secret. If he had an issue with the fact that his fatherhood had been known by all but him, he could only be angry with his ex-bride-to-be next door. But he felt slighted, in some way he couldn't explain, by the people he most trusted, if he trusted anyone at all anymore.

Of all the scenarios they'd plotted against him, this one felt the most personal and hurt the most. He wanted to be happy that he was going to be a father, but joy had not yet entered his heart. He felt that joy had been stolen from him.

He felt so crosswise and torn.

"How can we help you, Duke?" Pansy asked quietly. "This should be the happiest day of your life, actually."

He blinked. "I need to trust you."

"You can," Bug said.

"I can't," Duke said. "Especially not you two," he said to Pansy and Helen. "You're on Liberty's side."

"We're not on any side except the town's," Helen said.

"But I need you on mine, and you've always been against me. For me, but against me, in the most subtle way," he said. "If I'm going to catch that girl, I need utmost support, guidance and…well, no more keeping Duke in the dark."

Pansy shook her head. "Really, we're not counselors, Duke. We don't give advice."

"Nor support," Bug said, "not really."

"We're not exceptionally good with guidance," Mr. Parsons said. "We lean more toward incompetence. In all the years we've lived here, we haven't steered Tulips completely in the right direction. How could we steer you better?"

Duke looked at his office assistant and cellmate with some annoyance. "You're going to have to," he said with determination. "My stomach's in a knot, my heart feels like a boulder that could crack any second and my head's killing me. If this is fatherhood, I've got to get a grip. Soon."

Helen sniffed. "We just swore off all manner of helping and mollycoddling before you walked in. Mr. Parsons—Hiram—says we're the villains because we try to force our goodwill and guidance onto everyone."

Pansy nodded. "We've stunted the town by trying to over love it. So you're on your own, Duke, as much as we'd like to help you. We're giving up being villainesses."

He frowned at them. The little darlings were trying to weasel themselves out of their silver-haired duty and make him look like a clumsy, stumbling ox. "Oh, no, you don't. You are not going to leave me in my darkest hour and throw a melodramatic snit. That woman over there is having my child, and you're her mentors. You know more about her than anyone on this planet. All the fun and games are over." Pulling up a chair, he sat down between Pansy and Helen. "You're going to give me a crash course on winning a woman's heart, and we're going to do it in the next two weeks."

"Two weeks?" Helen repeated, startled. "It's not possible."

He leaned back, fully satisfied with his new position of power at the table. "Two weeks. I intend to wed my woman and have her completely thrilled about marrying me before my child is born." He gave them a satiric eyeing. "Because if not, should you try to thwart me in this, or even be unhelpful," he said sternly, "I'll move Liberty to the city. With me. And my child."

The two little darlings were fairly quivering with dismay, Duke saw with some amusement. He didn't mean a word of it, of course—but one had to wear the boots around here, and those two had been wearing the granny boots for too long.

Pansy straightened. "We certainly don't want that to happen, Duke," she said. "And in the spirit of cooperation, we've decided to let you in on our latest plan."

He raised an eyebrow, sensing a shift in the power struggle. "Oh?"

Pansy cleared her throat. "Valentine called a little while ago and said she had a wonderful idea." She sat forward, her face alight with excitement. "We want a reason for people to keep coming back to Tulips. And that would be *commerce*."

He smiled at Pansy, almost amused that she would use such a word. "So are we going to have a gingerbread sale? Maybe crochet some doilies and sell them at a sidewalk fair in the town square?"

Helen rapped his hand sharply. "Don't be such a goober, Duke. Surely you're hiding some brains under that hat of yours. We're going to have a rodeo."

He blinked. "A rodeo?"

"Yes," Pansy said, her face wreathed with delight, "with cowboys, cowboys and more cowboys!"

"Oh, swell," Duke said, "like the little fellow who was here today?" He recognized jealousy creeping into him again and told himself not to be a cretin.

"Precisely," Mr. Parsons said, "and I may get in the saddle myself, since the ladies like it so much."

Bug nodded. "Me, too."

They all looked at him. "Bug," Duke said, "Mrs. Carmine will be right put out with you if you go off cowboying, especially if some women start hanging on you."

"Gosh!" Bug blushed. "Mrs. Carmine will want to ride with me," he said defensively. "We're going to be the opening for the parade, since we have matched bays."

"Parade?" Duke shook his head. "We need an ordinance for a parade. There's been no ordinance come through my office."

They all looked at him, and Duke realized, slowly, of course, as if it almost had to seep through his hat into his skull, that his approval hadn't been required. This was another plot being hatched without him, only this plot wouldn't help him win Liberty at all. By including him, they were just trying to appease his pride. He'd never be able to trust these people—especially not where Liberty was concerned.

He stood. "I'll be seeing you. Good night, everyone."

Without another word, he left, letting the front door clap close behind him. Skirting Liberty's house—he didn't want to be tempted—he went the opposite way toward the sheriff's office.

He needed time to think. With a baby on the way he didn't have much time, and he wasn't as good at plotting as his townspeople were, so he needed to muster all of his powers of concentration.

It was going to be hard, because all his mind wanted to think about was Liberty, and his brain was still a little soft with the shock of impending fatherhood.

One thing was certain: he and Liberty were meant to be together. If the town mothers and fathers had decided that they were no longer dispensing advice—intending to make everyone more independent by not relying on them—he would stick to his new plan.

But nothing in that new plan included Liberty sitting in his office with his traitor dog by her side.

"Hi," he said, glad to see her but too surprised to admit it. "Change your mind?"

Chapter Seven

Liberty didn't blame Duke for being a bit sarcastic, but that didn't mean she was going to put up with it. "Do I have a reason to change my mind about anything?"

"No," he said, "but we could blame pregnancy hormones, if you wanted to change your mind and marry me like you should have in the first place."

Liberty could feel her temper rising. For the sake of their child—and because Duke had every reason to be upset with her—she collected herself. "I just want to offer an olive branch."

He shrugged. "None needed."

"Duke, I don't want to hurt you. That wasn't my intent. Maybe it was a mistake to come back, but I keep telling myself that it was the right thing to do for you and the baby."

"Where did you go, anyway, Liberty?" he asked, sliding a hip against his desk. "I don't quite have the time and location sequence straight in my mind."

She looked at him. "Are you asking me if I'm certain the baby is yours?"

He scowled at her. "I believe the question I asked was where you'd been during the time you were gone."

She blinked, realizing she'd been feeling defensive. "I was living in Dallas, working at a shop owned by a kind widow who felt the business was becoming too much for her. She loved my designs and we got along so well that once she found out I was pregnant—and single—she vowed to make my difficult situation a little easier. Next thing I knew she'd given the shop to me. Her generosity is something I will never forget."

Liberty cast her misty eyes down and Duke felt a moment of shame. Seems as if everywhere she went, people were happy to help her out and for that, he was grateful. Then he felt a twinge of anger— why wouldn't she let *him* make her life easier?

Liberty raised her head and continued. "I thought I would relocate the shop here, but then I realized my Dallas customer base would be better served in the current location. The shop has been there for many years."

"So you came back to Tulips just because of me? You didn't think I'd move to Dallas to be with my child?"

She looked at him. "It never crossed my mind to ask you to, Duke. You're happy here."

He crossed his arms and slid from the desk corner to pace for a moment. "You could have at least given me the option."

She sighed. "Your ranch is here, Duke. Your brother, and now your sister, and your job. All your friends. I could have asked you to move, but I didn't want to, and besides, it would have felt really strange to call you up and tell you that you were going to be a father and would you please uproot your life."

He looked at her. "Just for the record, it was a sacrifice you didn't need to make."

A frown touched her face. "I don't feel that I made any sacrifice. I gave up nothing. In fact, I only gained by coming back."

"What about your business?"

"I have two locations now, and the house I bought will be my office and central design area. I don't want to order everything. Some gowns will be my own private label called Liberty's Lace."

"That's pretty." He scratched at his chin. "Sounds like something you'd design."

She felt warmed by his praise. "And Holt is going to help me by creating fabulous bridal hairstyles so we can sell a whole wedding package. He does wonderful sketches of bride and gown—"

"I don't want to hear about Holt," Duke said. "As crazy as this sounds, I'm a bit jealous of him."

Liberty blinked. "Why?"

"Because he knows more about you than I do." Duke sighed. "There's no way for me to ever participate in your business."

"Oh, you wouldn't want to," Liberty said. "Hanging around a bunch of emotional brides would not be your thing, Duke. Really."

He shrugged, and she could tell she wasn't making him feel any better. In fact, the whole reason for her coming here was to make amends between them. She'd known she had wounded him and that had been her last desire. She wanted to repair the gulf between them.

"It feels strange to be expecting a child with you," she said, "and yet be so far apart from you."

"I know. This isn't something I'd ever envisioned happening."

She stood. "I'm sorry, Duke, I shouldn't have come—"

He swept her into his arms, giving her a kiss

that sent her head spinning and her heart craving more.

"You should always come to see me," he said. "Whether you like me or not, whether you think I should change or not, whether you think I'm a great guy or not—you should always talk to me whenever you want. Despite everything, we have this baby to raise now, and that means neither of us should stand on ceremony around each other."

She stared up at him, loving the feeling of his strong arms around her and the intense fire in his eyes as he gazed at her.

"Do we understand each other?" he asked huskily.

"Yes," Liberty said, pulling away, "we do." But her body didn't understand at all—didn't understand why she couldn't be in his arms forever. "Good night, Duke."

"'Night," he said, watching her leave as he gently patted Molly on her soft, squarish head.

So she left, a retreat of sorts, not exactly certain what had just happened between she and Duke. She wanted to go back to his office and say *I love you, really I do, I'm just scared about motherhood—and a little bit of you,* but her feet wouldn't move anywhere but back toward her house.

Molly came running to walk beside her, a gold

flash of fur and canine joy to be out in the September twilight. Liberty was happy to have the company until she got home.

But Molly-Jimbo wouldn't come inside her house. "If you come in, I'll sneak you one of Pansy's cookies."

The dog waved her tail and smiled up at Liberty from the porch—and then Liberty realized why. Molly's owner was standing beneath the trees that lined the front sidewalk, watching to make certain she got home safely.

Shivers broke over her skin. "Go home, Molly," she said softly, and the dog went running back to Duke. Tipping his hat to Liberty, he turned and walked off into the night.

Just like that. Protecting her as always. Looking after a citizen of Tulips.

Watching over his child.

Keeping Duke at arm's length was not going to be easy, Liberty realized. She'd been kidding herself that they might be partner-parents. It was going to be his way or no way, just as it always had been. He wasn't going to change at all. He couldn't. He was who he was, and as much as those character traits annoyed everyone, being strong was who he was.

Part of her was beginning to admire that strength, rather than feel trapped by it.

She had never been able to deny the fact that she loved Duke—but it was getting harder every day to ignore it. And if he didn't stop kissing her the way only Duke could kiss her, making her tingle all over and slightly crazy with desire, she was going to fall right back under his spell.

Chapter Eight

At the Triple F ranch, Pepper sat in the kitchen sketching out plans. Her brothers were gone for the moment and she had some time to hatch her thoughts, which were beginning to take shape in the few days since she'd been back to Tulips. She'd worried that Duke and Zach would pay her so much attention that she couldn't get any real planning done, but with Liberty's return to town, setting Duke's life ablaze, he'd left her alone.

Pepper wasn't the least bit interested in being anointed to Duke's personal throne—the sheriff's office. She had her own issues to think about, though home sweet home was never the place to come if one wanted to get away from issues.

Peace and quiet didn't usually last long in this town.

Eventually, she was going to do her bit to add

to the drama, Pepper thought, as she examined a list of empty buildings that Holt had given her. Thinking about her coming niece or nephew—she was going to be an aunt!—Pepper sighed. For a woman who'd been an undergrad at Princeton—pre-med with a business minor—then gone to med school at Tulane and finished third in her class, and who'd traveled much, she was in a tight spot.

Coming home had been the only way to pick the brambles and thorns from her conscience. Eventually, she was going to have to be as brave as Liberty had been about her circumstances.

But Duke Forrester was no Luke McGarrett—the only black knight in Pepper's entire life. Her one mistake. Even the smartest girls could fall for the baddest boys in town, and she certainly had.

She still thought about Luke, even their last hug. Some hugs stayed in your mind and resonated forever, stubbornly reminding you of what you'd once had.

She'd heard he'd become quite the playboy, which was not exactly an evolution that surprised her.

She picked up the phone and dialed a number. Her oldest son, Toby, answered, and just hearing his voice made the crease in her heart go away. "Hi, baby," she said.

"Hi, Mom." He sounded happy, which brought her relief. "Found us a house yet?"

"Got a list right here." She peered at Holt's list. "I'll be going to look today."

"Cool. Josh says to tell you Aunt Jerry is wearing him out."

Pepper laughed, knowing that was the highest of compliments from the twelve-year-old twins.

"Sorry, Mom, I have to go. Aunt Jerry's taking us to see a movie."

Pepper smiled. "Tell your brother I love him."

"Ew. I'll tell him you called. Bye, Mom!"

The phone clicked off. Pepper grinned as she hung up, feeling a twinge that she couldn't be there with her rambunctious sons.

But of course, they were the reason she was here in Tulips. Pepper looked at the paper again, then grabbed her car keys.

As long as Liberty kept Duke busy, Pepper figured she could have all the pieces in place by February—before anyone learned what she'd been hiding all these years. To confess her secret for her own benefit wouldn't be so difficult but it had yet to come to her how she was going to explain the boys.

Since they were the spitting image of Luke McGarrett, and people here had long memories, she knew she had to be careful. If she had their home, and hopefully her clinic, in place before she made her confession, perhaps they could hunker down for the storm.

Just the thought of Duke's reaction made her nervous. As soon as the truth was out, someone was going to call Luke McGarrett—and the plain fact was, selfish woman that she might be, she'd loved having her boys all to herself all these years.

She wasn't going to back down and she sure as hell wasn't going to apologize for what she'd done—but she by golly intended to be ready for the explosion.

ZACH SAT IN AN ancient live oak tree, staring down at the ground as he took a break from sawing limbs. He turned to gaze toward the main house on the Forrester property, thinking how nice it was that Pepper had come home. Duke wasn't around much now that Liberty had returned, and though his absence wasn't necessarily a bad thing, it was nice to have Pepper around to liven things up.

Of course, she wasn't as lively as she'd been when they were kids. But then maybe none of them were. Zach wiped away the sweat from his forehead, thinking about the women he was taking out tonight. Two dates, he'd bragged to Duke, but the reality was they were a couple of writers from another town who were keeping his secret: He was writing a western romance, packed with all of the things that he wasn't getting in Tulips these days. Love, sex, marriage. Not that he wanted to be married, not yet. Before that happened, he wanted to feel the *thunder*.

His greatest desire was to touch the flames of passion, catch lightning in a bottle.

So far, all he'd ever had was sex. Good sex, sure, but he needed to feel heat that would keep his jeans hot for weeks. He knew what he wanted, and it probably existed—somewhere—but writing about his desires was the next best thing.

He knew Duke would laugh him clean off the property if he knew.

"Duke doesn't know how good Duke has it," Zach said, venting his temper on a small limb. He sawed on it viciously until it fell to the ground. It was a satisfying sound, a swoosh of fulfillment, exactly what he needed to hear over and over again to keep himself from thinking about how much he coveted what his brother had.

Duke didn't appreciate anything. He had the girl, but he didn't get that right. He had the office, but he was mainly just a figurehead the townspeople tiptoed around.

"I'm moving a word processor in there, when

that office is mine," Zach muttered. "Mr. Parsons is getting put in a rent house so he can quit living off the city, and I'm bulldozing the Tulips Saloon to build an elementary school."

Another hunk of tree hit the ground after some concentrated attention from Zach's saw, and he rocked back to survey his handiwork. He hadn't put forth this scheme to usurp his brother, of course. In fact, being sheriff hadn't occurred to him until the ladies had approached him about taking over Duke's seat.

At first, he'd been troubled by the thought. Then he began to realize how much he could accomplish for the town. He had great ideas.

For once, he'd be the ambitious and innovative Forrester. After all, if the town was really to grow, they needed fewer teacups and more chalkboards. The tea parties could move to Liberty's white gingerbread house, right next to the gingerbread houses of Helen and Pansy.

He wasn't really being unkind, he told himself, just practical and businesslike. With change came progress.

Duke was going to be busy with Liberty and his new baby for a while, anyway. Too busy to interfere with Zach's plans. Zach slid down from the tree and landed on the ground, looking up at the pieces of sky he could see through the new spaces of the missing tree branches.

Change was good.

"No," DUKE TOLD the congregation standing around his desk, "I'm quite positive everything needs to just stay as it is for a while."

It had been a week since he'd last seen Liberty. They'd kept their distance from one another, though he'd caught a glimpse of her in church.

He suspected Liberty was taking pains to keep her distance from him, though he refused to be paranoid about it. In fact, everyone he knew was acting weird and secretive.

His nerves were beginning to twitch. He looked at Pansy and Helen, who'd dragged Holt along, and Bug. Duke wasn't certain if Mr. Parsons was in on the conference or had just come out of his cell to see what the hubbub was about. Of course, Liberty wasn't present.

Pansy made her appeal. "Duke, just because you have issues does not mean we can put the town's welfare on the back burner."

"That's right," Bug said. "You can make a decision, son."

"I'm not being indecisive," Duke said. "In fact, I'm being decisive by not making a decision.

Frankly, I think it's—" he swallowed the word *dumb* "—unnecessary to hold any type of big, disruptive event in Tulips. We'll grow when we're ready. The expense of holding a rodeo, parade, bachelorette ball or any other scheme you contrive isn't going to bring the commerce or settlers that you want to Tulips. I don't feel the expense is justified."

Helen looked annoyed. "I always hate talking to men about money. They're always so intent on being *justified*."

"It was so much easier with Sheriff Widow Gaines," Pansy said. "She didn't balk at new ideas as much as you do, Duke."

He sighed. "I'm not balking. Honestly, I'm not. And if you don't like my opinion, why did you come in here to get it?"

"Because we hoped to change your mind," Helen replied. "We hoped you'd see reason. Of course, I always forget that's about as likely as a donkey farting roses."

Duke blinked. "Bug, are you on their side? Do you think this rodeo is a good idea?"

"I am on no one's side," Bug said, making Duke think that if the man could be this politic in his marriage, maybe Mrs. Carmine wouldn't need to trawl him home every so often. "I feel that there are many things worth considering from both points of view."

"Well, can you split those trousers of yours any farther, Bug?" Mr. Parsons demanded. "You're blowing in the wind like a weather vane or a politician smoking something funny."

"I think the ladies have good points, and Duke makes fair points," Bug said defensively, "and it's judicious to consider all opinions. This isn't the 'Battle Of The Sexes.'"

They stared at him.

"Judicious?" Duke repeated.

"Well, Mr. Fair and Balanced," Pansy said, "I'll try to be more judicious the next time I'm baking chocolate chip cookies from scratch, alongside my famous rose-and-cranberry tea—"

"Okay, I admit it, I think the women are right," Bug said hurriedly. "Damn it, I tried. But they always win, Duke!"

Duke sighed, realizing he was putting everyone in a bad spot, most of all Bug, probably, who just wanted as much peace in his life as possible. "Okay, that's it. The answer is no. You want me to make a decision? I just did. The town doesn't need to change, except organically."

"What the hell does that mean?" Helen asked. "Organically?"

"It means," Duke said, "from whomever should move here—not be lured here. It means we grow on our own basic fundamentals instead of forcing it."

Pansy sighed. "Well, we'll have a growth of one this year, then. I suppose you could do us a favor and have twins, Duke."

"Twins?" He felt the blood drain from his face. "Mother always claimed twins ran in our family. But I'm pretty certain Liberty said there was only one baby we're expecting." He couldn't handle more shocks than had already been layered on him.

"Shoot," Holt said, "the ladies just want to have some type of social do. Can't you bend just once?"

Duke stared at the friend he'd known since childhood, and the man who trimmed his hair on the odd occasion Duke remembered to get it done. "I don't think so. It's a waste of valuable resources, mainly the money that the town has in its account."

"You know they're eventually going to have their way," Holt said.

"I know. They're going to vote Party Pepper and Zach-in-the-Box into the sheriff's position so they can have their way. But Tulips isn't Vegas," Duke pointed out.

"That's it!" Bug looked around. "A casino!"

"No!" they all chorused.

"Focus on organic growth," Duke reminded him. "From within. That's the way the best growth happens."

The group huddled for a minute, grumbling and whispering. Duke braced himself.

"So what about your own organic growth?" Mr. Parsons demanded. "If we have to wait nine months for every little bump in our census, can we at least be in on the process?"

"Well," Duke said slowly, "Liberty's busy. So I haven't talked to her."

"I don't think so," Pansy said innocently. "I saw her out weeding the garden yesterday."

"Weeding?" Was that the woman's version of *I didn't call because I had to wash my hair?*

"If you don't mind me saying so," Bug said, "and I hate to break rank here—Lord, I do, it's going to put me in a nonjudicious spot—but I put forth a motion to go around the sheriff."

They all stared at Bug.

"Well, if we have to wait on Duke, this town will never grow," Bug said, his arms crossed. "Son, you ain't got any get in your git-along."

"I second that," Mr. Parsons said. "I take his phone messages and Liberty hasn't called. We could all hit the time expiration on our meters of life if we wait on you, Duke. None of us are spring chickens, you know."

"Now, wait a second, folks," Duke said as they began filing out, "you're supposed to be preaching the gospel of the non-heady, non-rash approach to life that elderly people advise. We've all been happy moving at the pace of a snail!"

They didn't look back as they crossed the town square in unison toward the Tulips Saloon, the crucible of decisions he should probably never have given in on. "Saloon indeed," Duke mumbled. "More like a student coffeehouse or a hotbed of unrest and politicizing. Why can't you just be content to sit and sip tea like everyone else in your generation?" he called across to them. "Tea is excellent for the heart!"

They didn't turn around, and the stained-glass and wood doors closed, leaving him on the opposite side of the street.

"Ye gods," he muttered. "Molly!" He might as well go talk to Miss Green Thumbs, and Molly would be a great social prop.

But the dog didn't rush to his side and when he poked his head inside his office, he realized she'd slipped past him to follow Mr. Parsons. Turning, he watched her scratch at the Tulips Saloon door.

The door opened a crack, wide enough to let her flash in, and then it closed again.

He got the message. "That's it," he said, jamming his hat on his head. "My whole town is mutinying."

With two choices facing him—go home and face his chores or go to Liberty's and try to face his responsibilities—he opted for Miss Green Thumbs.

She wasn't in the yard weeding or growing anything, so he knocked on the door, his heart knocking nearly as loud inside him. A moment later, she opened the door, though she didn't smile when she saw it was him.

"Hi, Duke."

He nodded, trying to act as if his heart weren't playing a drum solo inside him. "Can I come in?"

"Sure," she said, and he walked inside, amazed at the change in her house.

"You don't waste any time. A week ago there were boxes everywhere."

"I don't like clutter and disorganization." She went into the kitchen, and he followed as she walked through into a smaller room. A wide, flat table was set up with a sewing mannequin nearby. On the table was Liberty's wedding gown—he knew it was. Nobody had to tell him because he'd thought about how she'd looked in that gown for seven months.

So when she sat down on a stool as if he weren't even there and picked up a seam ripper, loudly ripping out a long row of threads down the side of the gown, his hard-banging heart nearly exploded. "Liberty! What are you doing?"

She glanced up at him, her gaze steady.

"I'm taking my wedding gown apart," she said. "I won't be needing it anymore."

Chapter Nine

"In fact, I didn't need my gown in the first place," Liberty said with a frown, "since I apparently wasn't ready to marry. However, I've decided to donate it to someone who is very ready."

"Donate it!" Duke's skin turned pale.

"Are you all right?" she asked, concerned. "Why don't you sit on this stool, Duke?"

He sat, but he wasn't happy. "Liberty, you need to be wearing that gown, not donating it."

"Oh," she said, looking at it. "Duke, I'd rather give it away. The girl I'm giving it to is an unwed mother in Dallas whose boyfriend has decided he wants nothing more than to marry her. I'd like her to have something special to wear. She's such a sweet girl."

Sighing, he said, "You probably own the only

wedding shop that donates gowns. Specifically your own."

"For the record," Liberty said, "my business operates very much in the black, thank you. Second, this is the only time I've done this. I could have sold it on eBay, or I could have sold it secondhand in Dallas, but I saw this girl peering in the window, and I…"

He frowned at her. "Go on. I'm listening."

She raised her chin. "I saw myself in her. She would never have dreamed of having something so pretty. It was obvious that she was expecting a baby." Her gaze held his defiantly. "I really don't have to explain myself."

"No, you don't."

"But I don't mean to upset you."

"Upset? How else should I feel?" he asked her. "I'm not exactly delighted to see the woman I nearly married ripping up her gown. I'm sure I'm behaving normally, though everyone in this town is trying to convince me otherwise."

"Okay. You have a point." She put down the seam ripper. "Duke, I made this gown with my own hands. It makes me happy that someone who can use it will look lovely on her own special day. Frankly, it was hanging in my closet like an unhappy ghost of weddings past, and I really want to move beyond all those feelings."

"Yeah." He scratched his head and stood. "So do I."

They looked at each other for a long moment, and Liberty realized Duke misunderstood her. "I don't regard what we did as a mistake."

"You sure sound like you do."

"Come on." Taking him by the hand, she pulled him from the sewing room. "We can talk better out here."

"Personally, I think we've done enough talking. That's all anybody does in this town is talk. Yakkity-yak-yak. But nothing really gets said! Have you noticed that? If we could bottle all the hot air around here, we could melt the polar ice caps with it."

She looked at him, assessing the lines around his mouth and the grooves near his eyes. Had they been there before? "Do you feel well?"

He shrugged. "Guess as well as can be expected."

She nodded. "Okay."

"How are you feeling?"

"I feel wonderful. Better than I ever have in my life." She smiled. "I love being pregnant."

He grunted. "Glad to be of service."

Seated upon the sofa, he looked stiff and out of

place in the fancy parlor room. Liberty realized she'd intended this room to be a reception area of sorts, for any visitors, business or otherwise, who stopped by, but Duke no more fit this room than the sewing room. "You don't look comfortable," she said. "Let's move you to the kitchen."

But there wasn't a bar stool or a table in there yet. He seemed big and cramped in the small kitchen. And still awkward. "You just don't fit in this house."

"I know," he said. "I knew that when you told me you'd bought it. So that was fine, but then I started thinking about how you're going to raise a baby in this house."

She smiled. "Children are raised in much smaller dwellings, Duke. Not every child grows up on a place the size of the Triple F ranch. Besides, it's all about the love in the home."

"Yeah." He looked happier about that.

"So, was there a particular reason you stopped by?"

"The old ladies are after me," he said. "They've denied me their approval ever since you returned, and it's starting to hurt my feelings."

Liberty laughed. "They are dears."

"I don't think so. My opinion is that they're tyrants, and they like it that way."

"They're your best friends. I've just set everybody on edge," Liberty said, knowing it was true and feeling worse for it. "I'm so sorry, Duke. I really didn't know that they'd take sides the way they have, at your expense. I certainly didn't want that to happen." She gave him a peacemaking smile, thinking he really was the most handsome man she'd ever seen. "Duke, they just love you so much. They treat you like a son."

His eyebrows rose. "I want *you* to love me so much."

She hesitated, not about to tell him that she did. Nothing between them would change, so why get caught in that which would only lead to pain later? And even more so for their child? "I don't regret that we wanted to get married," she said carefully. "We both believed we were in love, and we both felt strongly about that. It's a memory I treasure."

"Yeah, well, I'm not going to try to pretend that I don't love you anymore, because I do." He stuck his chin out, a stubborn trait she remembered too well. "And I believe you're showing, Miss Wentworth."

"Showing what?"

"Showing just what my love for you did to you," he said proudly. "You'd need a much bigger wedding gown now."

She wrinkled her nose. "Of course I've gained weight. I have our baby growing inside me."

"You're very attractive as an expectant mother, Miss Wentworth. Have the ladies of the saloon been taking care of your gastronomic health?"

"They bake me cookies, yes. Make sure I'm taking my vitamins."

He grinned. "Those little blue-haired friends of ours have been taking very good care of their girl, I believe. I'll have to thank them for that." Putting on his hat, he gave her belly a last, satisfied glance. "You're quite curvaceous, my sweet, like a happy pumpkin in a patch."

"Duke," Liberty said, following him as he strode to the door like a conquering lord, "my stomach is nowhere the size of your head."

He turned and grinned, unaffected by her retort. "You're beautiful, pumpkin."

"That's not funny," she told him, but he kissed her forehead and left.

That bothered her more than anything. A kiss on the forehead? Duke had never failed to romance her lips every chance he got. Now she was the recipient of a brotherly peck?

"I don't like it," she called to him.

On the sidewalk, he turned to look back at her.

"The complaint desk is open. Lodge your complaint."

"I never did like your stubborn side," she said, "and I don't want you kissing me." Not on the forehead, anyway.

He shrugged. "The complaint desk is now closed."

She watched him walk on, and heard him whistling a happy tune. He wasn't going to change, she realized; it was always going to be his way or no way.

The waiting game she was playing was a dangerous one.

If she thought Duke was going to realize that he intimidated people by being such a jock, such a man, such a meathead, she was destined to be disappointed. The man simply thought he was right about everything. "Your father is a…wonderful man," she told her baby, rubbing her stomach. "You're the luckiest baby."

Her stomach rolled with a sudden cramp, as if the baby were kicking an agreement. The cramp turned dull and throbbed. Liberty went inside, returning to the wedding gown she'd been taking apart.

It was a beautiful dress, but it no longer represented all of her dreams. It was the gown of someone else's dreams now, and Liberty was delighted that she could give it to someone less fortunate. Maybe, just maybe, it would make her future a wonderfully romantic one to match the hope and dreams she'd seen in the young girl's eyes.

Her eyes had held those stars once.

The cramps came again. Liberty breathed slowly, telling herself to relax before beginning to repin the seams. If it took all night, she was determined to finish this job—and she wasn't going to think about Duke at all.

Or at least, not much.

IF LIBERTY THOUGHT Duke was going to sit in his office and ignore the fact that she'd made him a father, she was in for a surprise. Nothing had changed at all for him—not his love for her, nor his desire to marry her. And the sooner, the better.

Very likely the only way to achieve his goal of spending the rest of his life with Liberty was through a different avenue, one heretofore unchartered. The Tulips Saloon Gang was not on his side, but they easily could be, he thought, with a little prodding.

Since he was a man, and since he'd always engaged in a wee bit of cat-and-mouse with the ladies, his request for assistance might meet with a brick wall of sorts. But a big idea had come to him—which was that no woman could resist a man who honestly loved her, and that would include the women of the Tulips Saloon. He needed them on his team.

If he had a good old-fashioned hen session with them—as much as it would grate against his principles to do so—they would realize that they were on the wrong side. "So, hennies, here I come," he muttered, adjusting his hat for courage as he broached the saloon door.

Pansy and Helen were laying out new tablecloths. Fall colors, with rich burgundies and plums and some evergreen. "Hello, Sheriff," Helen said. "You're just in time to help us."

So he helped them spread out tablecloths, and when every table was ready for business the next day, Duke cleared his throat. "If you have a moment, Miss Helen, Miss Pansy, I sure could use your advice. Even though you're not giving advice anymore," he said, feeling quite cagey, "this is more of a personal matter."

"Oh," Pansy said, and he saw the interest lighting her eyes. Helen wasn't immune, either, and he saw her objections faltering.

He took off his hat, holding it in his hands. "I don't think Liberty loves me anymore."

"Oh-h-h," Helen and Pansy said. Pansy patted

his shoulder and pressed him into a chair, and Helen placed a teacup into his hands.

He sighed, smiling inwardly. He was in! Just like Holt, he was going to get a hen session with the ladies!

It almost felt good—and not sissy at all.

"I'm sure she loves you," Pansy said, sitting next to him. "She just learned to live without you."

That wasn't what he'd come to hear. He felt his eyebrows furrowing together and made certain he wiped the frown away. "Of course, I don't want my child to learn to live without me. I want to be a big part of its life."

"That's why Liberty moved back," Helen said. "She knew you'd feel that way. Everybody knows you'd want to be with your child, Duke. You're a good man."

"So that brings us back to Liberty," he said, making his way back to the subject that most interested him. "I want to be with her, too. We belong together. As a family, and as man and wife."

Pansy sighed. "I don't think that will happen, Duke."

Helen shook her head.

He couldn't help the frown that jumped onto his face now. "I don't understand why, though.

How can she be carrying my child and not want to marry me?"

"Women do that all the time," Pansy said. "Sometimes men are too much trouble."

"Women are too much trouble," Duke said. "She's the one who's being ornery!"

Helen shook her head. "Although I try not to take sides, I do understand that you can be quite intimidating, Duke."

"You need a more…submissive type of girl," Pansy offered. "One who doesn't mind a man running everything for her. There are lots of—"

"I need Liberty!" he stated, not meaning to roar but realizing he'd gotten a little loud from the dismayed expression on the ladies' faces. "Oh, damn it. I mean darn it. I mean…don't start getting all puckered on me. I'm not trying to hurt your feelings. I swear, everyone in this town is as delicate as a china cup."

"And you're pretty much our bull in the china shop," Pansy offered, her voice soft and hesitant. "Though we do love you. But you do have a tendency to roughness."

He sighed. "I don't remember any of you mentioning that before. I have never raised my voice to a woman. If I get a cat's whisker above what it would take for a mouse to hear me, you two act like I'm at a college keg party. I haven't had a chance in my life to be rowdy around women, because either you or my mother was always after me to be certain that I was a gentleman."

"But as we said, we love you anyway, though we're not certain where you got your rascal side," Helen said.

He shook his head. "So where do I stand with Liberty?"

"Well, you'll always be connected through that little dumpling you're going to have in a couple of months," Pansy said. "That's the bright side. It's just such a shame you don't handle change better."

"Change? I handle change just fine."

Helen shook her head. "You have never liked anything of the sort, Duke, from the time you were a child. You don't want to change, you don't want us to change, you don't want the town to change. And then Liberty changed on you, and…well, it's an unfortunate problem you have." She looked very sad about that.

He put his hat back on, completely dissatisfied with his "hen session." If he didn't know better, he'd think he was no better off than when he'd come in.

"Guess I'll go with the bright side, then," he said, not feeling brighter at all. "Thanks, ladies."

Pansy leaned up to give him a peck on the cheek.

"We'll ruminate on your dilemma some more, Duke. Maybe we can come up with something."

"Thanks." He perked up. "I'd appreciate that."

Helen smiled and gave him a hug as she stared up at him. He loved these two women, he really did. They might be the bane of his existence, but without them, his life would be very dull. They kept him sharp, focused.

"You really do love her, don't you?" Helen asked.

"Yes, ma'am, I do," he said. "Always have, always will."

They smiled at him. Duke left, wondering why he always had to be the one to prove how much he loved Liberty, then realized he didn't care. If he had to say it every day, if he had to shout it from the roof of the Tulips Saloon, then he'd do that.

Although he wasn't certain Liberty was in a listening mood.

At the jail, Bug Carmine was sitting in the cell with Mr. Parsons. The two of them were tweaking some coiled wires that were connected to a black box. Duke sat in his chair. "Fellows, what trouble are you getting into now?

"Not the kind of trouble you're in," Mr. Parsons said.

Duke frowned. "What does that mean?"

"It means Liberty just called. She said to tell you that she's going into Dallas to fit a gown on a bride."

"Why does that mean trouble for me?" Duke asked. "Liberty's free to do as she likes."

Bug got up. "In my house, it's the man that does the departing."

Duke and Mr. Parsons stared at him. "First of all," Duke said, "that sounded slightly male chauvinistic, which I'm always getting in trouble for in this town, and yet, I believe that statement has anything I've ever said beat. Second, you and Mrs. Carmine are married. Liberty and I are not. She called me, and that alone was more than she had to do, as much as that pains me to say it." He grimaced.

"Well, that's not where the trouble comes in," Bug said helpfully. "That was just the warm-up."

Duke sighed. "So?"

"Your sister called. She bought a building in town."

"A building?" Duke shook his head. "Why would she do that? We have plenty of room at the ranch."

"This is for a clinic," Mr. Parsons said helpfully. "I know, because it's information that will have to go in the file."

"Which file?" Duke asked carefully. "I'm still

a bit confused on the filing system in my office. It's a problem I intend to sort out soon."

"Why, the appropriate file," Mr. Parsons said, amazed that Duke couldn't understand such a simple system. "And your brother called. He said he'd be gone for the evening with a pair of twins from another town. He sounded extremely happy about that."

Duke shook his head. "And the old ladies beat me up for being a rascal."

"Well," Bug said, "as interesting as that was, I've got something to do." He stood, and Duke noticed he was holding a brown paper bag.

"Excuse me, Bug," he said, "but I don't think it's your time of the month, is it?"

"Pardon me?" Bug asked. "I'm not a woman. I don't have *times* of the month. And for your information, Mrs. Carmine has gone to see her sister. I'm a free man and can do what I please. Within reason, naturally."

Duke didn't think that sounded like a good idea. Though he still had Bug's firearm, Bug going off without Mrs. Carmine to keep an ear out for him felt wrong. "I'll come with you," Duke said.

"I could use the company," Bug said, "if you don't talk too much."

Duke put on his hat. "I don't want to talk at all."

"Bye, Hiram," Bug said, "and Jimbo."

"Her name is Molly," Duke said as he followed Bug out.

"You said you'd be quiet," Bug reminded him. "This is my quiet time. It's when I *focus*."

"Sheesh, Bug, it's not like your wife is exactly loquacious," Duke muttered, trying to sound sarcastic in a halfhearted way. What was wrong with all the people in this town? Everybody wanted to be so difficult—except him. He really felt as if he were the easy sort among a population of troublemakers.

Bug rounded on him. "Look, if you're going to chatter like a girl at a dance—"

Duke held up a hand. "I promise not to say a word."

THIRTY MINUTES LATER, he and Bug were staring at the sky in a remote field. After a few healthy swigs of Bug's tonic—and then a few more—Duke was glad it was September, didn't care so much that Liberty wouldn't marry him and had nearly convinced himself that fatherhood wasn't scaring the tar out of him. "It's change," Duke says. "Change apparently bothers me."

"Well, hell, yeah," Bug said. "No man likes change. We're supposed to be the stable ones.

How can we be stable if women are always running around diddling with everything? It's like lining up the cosmos and then whacking it with a pool cue and sending little balls of change flying everywhere." He took another drink. "No. A man has enough trouble with a woman, because she for sure brings every kind of upset he'll ever want to meet into his life. Look at you, for example."

"Yeah, look at me," Duke said, feeling glad to be getting some sympathy for once.

"Liberty's changing you," Bug said. "You used to be fun."

"I'm sitting here drinking with you," Duke said. "How the hell am I not being fun?"

"I don't know," Bug said, "you're just not. Ever since Liberty returned, you've been a pain in the ass. In fact, I think the ladies voted to give you a vacation."

Duke wrinkled his forehead and moved his hat under his head to a more comfortable position. "What kind of vacation?"

"Something about a permanent vacation," Bug said, "but I wasn't listening."

"I don't care," Duke said. "Not anymore. It would be the change I need." He closed his eyes. "See, I can change just fine."

"Well, I don't know about that," Bug said.

"Change is no good." After a moment, he let out a soft snore. Duke took a deep breath, wishing he was with Liberty instead of babysitting Bug. Liberty was softer, she smelled good and he didn't think she snored. But even if she did, he wouldn't give a damn as long as he could sleep with her every night.

"Duke Forrester!" he heard suddenly. He sat up, confused, staring up into the sun.

After his eyes adjusted, he realized Pansy and Helen were standing in front of him, their little hands on their hips, staring at him as if he were the greatest disappointment they'd ever seen.

"Yes, ma'am? Ma'ams?"

Beside him, Bug sat up, too, and rubbed his eyes. "What's going on? This is my quiet time, damn it!"

"Bug, you got Duke drunk!" Helen accused.

"I did not!" Bug said. "He invited himself along!"

Duke got to his feet. "How did you find us?"

"Mr. Parsons told us where you'd gone and with what," Pansy said, her tone gently reproving. "Honestly, Duke, this isn't how you plan to act when you become a father, is it?"

"Bug Carmine, don't you dare teach Duke your bad habit," Helen demanded. "Going off like that is just plain irresponsible!"

"I had time on my hands," Duke said. "Liberty went to Dallas. I was trying to get my mind off it." He didn't say that he thought he was doing the right thing by keeping an eye on Bug because he didn't want to bring any wrath on the elderly man.

"I was just trying to keep him from thinking about Liberty," Bug said. "Lord, he just about talked my ear off about her the entire time we've been here. I could barely get any rest at all."

"Rest?" Helen said. "Bug, if you get any more rested, you're likely to stay asleep for good."

Pansy sniffed. "Let's go, Helen. Duke obviously doesn't need our help after all."

"Help?" Duke began tagging along after the ladies—escorting them to their vehicle, he told himself—feeling no reason to be loyal and hang back with Bug the Rat. Sometimes brotherhood and the bachelor life weren't what they were cracked up to be. "What kind of help?"

"Help with Liberty," Pansy said, her little mouth drawn up into a bow of disapproval that she mostly reserved for Bug. Then she brightened. "Though we remind you that it's taking a chance because we don't think our ratio of success in giving advice is all that it could be. But we have a plan. You might call it a recipe."

"But first you'd have to be willing to change,"

Helen said, and Duke knew he had reached the point of no return.

It was now or never.

Chapter Ten

Liberty drove back from Dallas, feeling satisfied with the results of her wedding gown project. It had fit her customer perfectly, and the young girl was ecstatic and grateful. That was the way a wedding gown should make a woman feel, and as she parked and walked inside her house, Liberty knew she'd discovered what had been bothering her.

She hadn't felt ecstatic about the idea of marrying Duke. The exact wording of the problem had eluded her until now, but the fact was, once she'd given in to the fear, she'd erased all the sensations of joy that should surround the holy blessing of marriage.

It wasn't Duke's fault. It was hers. She was the one who didn't recognize at first that being with a man with such an unyielding idea of what a woman should be would be too much for her to live with for the rest of her life. Rubbing her stomach, Liberty went inside, waiting for the cramps to pass. Pansy and Helen had said maybe the cramps were Braxton-Hicks contractions, or maybe baby-growing pains, but they thought she should make an appointment with her doctor. She had, though she hadn't informed Duke.

She knew that he would move right in with her if he even half suspected she might be having problems. And if he knew she was just the teensiest bit apprehensive about her pregnancy, Liberty knew he'd be right by her side.

Actually, that sounded wonderful in a way. Heavenly. One thing about Duke that she could never resist was his undying loyalty, and his shirt-off-my-back generosity. He was one of the most unselfish people she had ever met.

He was so much like his parents in that regard. Liberty went into the kitchen, finding a message on her answering machine. She pressed Play.

"Liberty," Pansy's voice said, "call me. Helen and I want to talk to you about a little plan we've been mulling over."

Liberty smiled. Those two ladies were her best friends, and they were always into something, which made them fun. All her life she'd ached for the love of a mother's attention, and when those two had decided to make a case of her, she had never lacked for friendship again.

Except Duke's, of course, but that had been her own choosing.

"WE DIDN'T MEAN TO BE harsh on you earlier," Helen said as she, Duke and Pansy sat in the Tulips Saloon. After making certain Bug was safely home—he'd thrown his bottle away, claiming that Duke had completely ruined the experience for him—the three of them had gone to the saloon. It was the best place for what they had to say, Helen had claimed, and Duke had to admit he felt pretty happy about getting his own private invitation into their world. All of that barging in was starting to get tiring.

"We didn't mean to send you away without being helpful," Pansy said. "It's just that these days we've lost confidence in our ability to be helpful the way we want to be."

Duke sat on the velvet-covered antique chair he'd been assigned and gratefully accepted the lavender tea Pansy gave him. Okay, it was a bit sweet for his black-coffee-loving soul. Yet he craved the warmth these women brought to his life. He took a big swig. "Better than Bug's juice," he said, reaping a smile of approval from Helen.

"Frankly, I think the only people on this planet who can help me with Liberty are you two."

"Well," Helen said, sitting across from him, "this is a recipe." She pulled a paper from her purse.

"Oh." He set his delicate teacup down on the pie table next to him. "I don't cook."

"You have to change," Pansy said.

Duke raised his eyebrows. "Cooking will help me convince Liberty that I'm the only man for her?"

"No," Helen said, "but unless you change, you'll have to forget about her."

"I can change," Duke said. "Give me a pot or a pan."

The ladies smiled. "This isn't an ordinary recipe we're giving you," Helen said. "You'll have to be very careful with the ingredients."

He frowned. Were they trying to work him into a corral? They were tricky ladies and there had been an undeclared war between Duke and them for the past couple of years. They'd been known to spring a trap or two on him, all in the spirit of fun. He gazed at each of them in turn and decided that this time it seemed they had his interest in mind. "All right. I can be careful."

"Very gentle," Pansy said. "No bull in a china shop."

"I really don't try to be," Duke said, his feelings a trifle hurt. "I can't help that I'm big, and strong, and—"

"Yes, yes," Helen said, as he began to warm to his favorite subject. "But still a man must be very gentle, Duke. We're all aware of your manly attributes. We think you're a fine sheriff."

"Well, that's the first time you've said that," he said, allowing himself a slight grumble at their expense.

"But we want you to work on your feminine side," Pansy said.

He blinked. "Look, I like Holt as much as you do, he's like a brother, but I can't move very far away from my side of the fence."

"You have this all wrong," Helen said. "Which means we have a lot of work to do if you want to get your girl. And I don't know that you can," she said with a sniff. "This is all quite dicey."

"I think he's had enough for today," Pansy said. "Why don't we just give him the recipe and allow him to digest the ingredients on his own. Then if he has any questions, he can come ask us."

Helen looked at him for a long time. He felt strangely, as if he'd failed his old and gentle friends. "I'm sorry," he said. "I do love Liberty. I'd give her the moon. But there's only so many tricks this old dog can learn."

Helen and Pansy looked at each other for a moment. Silently, Helen handed Duke a sealed envelope. "We love you, Duke," she said. "We hope you can work it out."

He had fallen short of the mark, been dismissed from this hen session. Sadly, Duke rose. "Thank you," he said, giving them both a hug. "I love you both."

Putting his envelope in his pocket, he left. He'd had a little Bug advice and now a little Helen-Pansy time, and he should be feeling as if he had this Liberty problem in hand.

Yet he felt as if he were further than ever from getting his lady to the altar.

"YOU SEE, DEAR," Helen said to Liberty as they sat in her parlor, "we think change is a wonderful component in a person's life."

"Yes," Pansy said, "like sewing a different color of sequins on a gown. It can make all the difference in the world, don't you agree?"

"I do," Liberty said. "Change can be positive."

Helen smiled. "We were hoping you'd feel that way."

"Oh?" Liberty took some cookies from a bag and laid them on a plate. "These aren't homemade—"

"They're fine," Pansy said, taking one and placing it on a china saucer. "We brought you a recipe."

"A recipe?" Liberty asked. "I thought we were talking about change."

"We are, dear," Helen said. "That's what this recipe is for."

She handed her a pretty envelope and Liberty smiled. "You're trying to get me to take back Duke."

"Yes, dear," Pansy said, quite unashamed. "We think perhaps you're going about catching that cowboy all wrong."

"Yes," Helen said, "we want you to be happy. And all this drama is upsetting the equilibrium of Tulips. Tulips, you know, is always our greatest concern."

"But Duke and I are not right for each other." Liberty looked at them. "We'd end up like Bug and Mrs. Carmine. He'd regret marrying me. I know he would. Duke is the impenetrable rock, and I'm more like water."

"Yes," Helen said, "but what if Duke made a wee adjustment?"

"I'm not trying to change him," Liberty said. "I want him to be happy. That's why I left him."

"The only way he's ever going to be happy is with you," Pansy told her kindly. "He's tried everything to make you happy, from leaving you be, to pestering you, but we think there's another way. If you take the first step, it would probably start a chain reaction."

"I don't know," Liberty said, thinking about ecstatic happiness. "Shouldn't it be easier than that?"

"Only in Hollywood," Helen told her.

"Be brave," Pansy said. "You're a go-getter type of girl. Get your man, for heaven's sake!"

Liberty hesitated. "What did you have in mind?"

"A recipe," Helen said, "in that envelope. We give it to you with one caveat—we could be very wrong about the ingredients."

"It's not foolproof, in other words," Pansy said. "But it's the best we could come up with."

"Put like that, I guess I'll try a new recipe," Liberty said, and the ladies rose.

"We love you, Liberty," they said, hugging her. "Are you still having that tiny tummyache?"

"Just slightly," Liberty said. "Don't worry about me."

"We worry all the time," Pansy said. "That's sort of what mothers do. If we *were* your mother, which we're not, but still we worry like that."

"Yes, well, come on, Pansy," Helen said. "Liberty can't 'cook' with us standing here bothering her. Good night, Liberty!"

They left, and Liberty smiled at the pretty envelope. It was on Tulips stationary with the red and hot-pink flowers in abundance, just like the front door of the saloon. Duke had helped them hang that door, and he'd complained every second that it would never stand up to everyday abuse. The colored glass, he said, would eventually get damaged.

But after it was hung, he'd told them it was beautiful. That was Duke, resisting change, and then being big enough to admit someone else was right.

She could change, she decided, putting a hand against her stomach. She had reason to. In her heart, she knew she loved Duke. He would be a wonderful father, too.

Fear was no reason to keep someone out of her life. It wasn't going to be the way it had been with her parents; there would be no neglect, there would be no waking up one day and finding they'd moved to a faraway place.

Mr. and Mrs. Forrester, who had basically taken her in, would be pleased that she was a true Forrester. She missed them. It was true that after they'd passed away, Duke had become a harder, more self-reliant person. She was drawn to his strength.

She shouldn't be afraid of loving, or loving him in particular.

She should be ecstatic.

Slowly, she opened the tulips-printed envelope.

DUKE STARED at the recipe. It was written on pretty paper in Pansy's fine hand, but it was Helen's spicy title, he was certain.

A Simple Recipe For Winning Your Woman.

"Lovely," he told Molly-Jimbo as she laid her head on his leg. They sat together companionably in his office. Mr. Parsons was out, though the copper box rested in its corner, Duke noticed. One day he was going to convince the old man to put the box inside a safe somewhere. "Helen says this is a simple recipe, Molly. That sweet lady doesn't think I can handle anything hard."

Smiling at their whimsy, he moved his gaze down to the first ingredient.

Step One: Be kind. Romantic. Gentle. Think of days gone by. Try whispering instead of yelling; old movies instead of sex.

"Ugh," Duke said, "they don't ask much of a man, do they?"

Molly let out a whoosh of breath but he didn't think she was agreeing with his sarcasm. Old movies instead of sex! How much change was he supposed to endure? Days gone by? How was a man supposed to be a man—and a sheriff—if he was soft all the time? "Their little tatted doilies have gone to their heads," Duke said, "like spidery webs of nonsense."

Was this what Liberty wanted, though? Did they have a point? They were women. Surely women knew what other women wanted. He rubbed at his chin. "I think they're working me like a dog," he told Molly, who closed her eyes. "This isn't the kind of advice I need." Putting away the recipe, he stood, gazing through the bars of Mr. Parsons's cell at the copper box.

But being the same bullheaded sheriff hadn't gotten him anywhere with the woman he loved, had it? There were lots of things he didn't know about a lot of people, he decided. And if Liberty wanted romance, then he could certainly give this recipe a shot. And since he was a man of action, he marched toward Liberty's directly.

A few minutes later, he stood on her porch, took a deep breath and rang the bell.

She opened the door, looking more beautiful than he'd ever seen her. "Hi," he said, unable to come up with something more creative.

"Come in," she said. She was dressed in a bathrobe and something delicious-smelling was in the oven. His senses were overwhelmed by all the things he loved about Liberty.

But he hadn't come there to eat, or even just to

gawk at this gorgeous woman. Before he could chicken out, he walked inside the house. "I know I should have called first, but then I'd lose my nerve."

"Your nerve?" She stared at him. "That's something I never worry about you losing, Duke."

Well, she would be very surprised if she knew that his insides were quivering like some of Pansy's Jell-O molds. "Liberty," he said, drawing a deep breath, "I…I am looking forward to having a baby with you."

She didn't say a word, but he thought he might be going in the right direction since he detected a softening around her eyes. Touching the recipe in his pocket for courage, and careful to keep his tone gentle, he said, "One day maybe we could watch a movie together. Rent one, maybe, one of those oldies but goodies."

The smile he'd been hoping for bloomed. "That sounds nice, Duke. I'm baking a cake for the ladies. They'll be here soon to help fit me for a new maternity dress, but I can sneak you a piece of pound cake. If you'd like some."

Duke made a mental note to run through a guide of old movies very soon. "I'd love some."

"You sit down." Liberty gestured to the kitchen table. "Would you like milk with that?" she asked, turning her back so that she could snatch a note from her pocket. *A Recipe For Romancing Your Stubborn Sheriff* was scrolled across the top in Pansy's pretty writing. Taking a deep breath, Liberty quickly read the first "tip" of the recipe.

Smile and be of good cheer, but also, keep your "gown" down.

Not an easy "ingredient" to follow! She and Duke had enjoyed making love, and even a simple touch had always ignited fireworks between them. This new awkward formality between them didn't feel anything but forced—and yet, the situation they were in was difficult.

Never being touched by Duke again wasn't what her heart wanted, even if her mind and practical nature overwhelmed her innermost feelings. He was a sexy man, and she'd never been able to tell him no—except at the altar. How could she love him so much and know they could never live together and be happy?

Maybe she had been the one who'd needed to change.

"Is everything all right?" Duke asked, and Liberty whirled around.

"It's fine. I'm sorry, Duke." She quickly cut a

piece of cake and laid it in front of him, but he caught her hand as she put the plate down.

"You look beautiful, Libby," he said. "I miss you."

She stopped, caught by the fire in his gaze. "Even as round as I am?" she asked softly.

A slow, hot grin lit his face. "I've never seen you sexier."

She heard scratching at the door and backed away from him, her heart racing. "I believe that would be the other woman in your life," she said. "I'll let her in."

She wasn't surprised when Molly made a bee-line for Duke and the kitchen. She heard Duke laugh.

"So the smell of cake called you home like Lassie," Duke told the dog. "You're a faithless cur." He fed her a tiny bite with an apologetic shrug at Liberty. "She won't leave crumbs on your floor."

"I can sweep if she does."

Duke looked down at his dog. "Dogs really don't eat cake," he told her. "Men don't sweep up after dogs if they make a mess eating cake."

"Men do sweep," Liberty said, and Duke nodded, still looking at his cake-eating dog with some resignation.

"For you, Liberty, I would sweep," Duke

said. He couldn't help adding, "but I guess a gentleman doesn't sweep a lady off her feet and make love to her."

The doorbell rang almost as loud as the sudden beating of Liberty's heart. She remembered making love with Duke—she remembered feeling that nothing and no one could ever keep them apart.

Except a baby, Liberty thought unexpectedly. *I don't want Duke romancing me because of the baby!*

She suddenly felt the ache in her abdomen return. "That's Pansy and Helen. Eat and tell me if I got the recipe right."

"It's perfect!" She heard his words as she fled the kitchen and escaped the heat of his eyes.

"Okay, forget 'down,' my gown was in great danger of coming off," she muttered, opening the door to her friends with some relief.

"Mmm, pound cake," Helen said, and Liberty hugged her. "I've been looking forward to this all day."

"I have a sheriff in the kitchen with a big piece," Liberty said, hugging Pansy.

"Piece?" Pansy asked. "Doesn't Duke always carry a gun? Or were you speaking metaphysically?"

"Cake," Liberty said with a sigh. "You certainly

have a fanciful mind, Pansy. By the way, your recipe was very helpful."

"I didn't give you a pound cake recipe," Pansy said. "My pound cake comes out like a brick."

"She meant *the* recipe," Helen said, nudging her friend.

"Oh," Pansy said, her face lighting up. "You think we might be giving good advice for a change?"

"I don't know," Liberty said. "I didn't get past the first ingredient. Just staying calm around Duke is a feat for me. So I smiled and—"

"And obviously you're dressed," Helen said with a sniff.

"Yes," Pansy said, "we feel that a man who gets the milk from the cow—"

"No," Helen said, "we're too far past that. The cow is long gone and in the process of having a calf." She smiled at Liberty. "We're hoping better communication between you two, some easy camaraderie, might break the ice that's been forming ever since you returned."

"Ladies," Duke said, tipping his hat as he walked into the foyer. "It's good to see you, but I must be off."

"Must you go, Duke?" Pansy asked. "We don't mean to run you out. We just have a little pinning and tucking to do."

He shook his head. "The cake was delicious," he told Liberty, and kissed her square on the lips, surprising all three women into silence. "Let's watch that movie soon," he said, and walked out.

The click of the door closing behind him was deafening.

Helen blinked. "Well!"

Pansy giggled. "He reminds me of Cary Grant. I do believe he was trying to act suave and debonair."

Liberty's lips still tingled from the kiss he'd landed on her. For a quick peck, he'd managed to impart an awful lot of "want you" into it! "That wasn't like Duke at all. He's never done anything like that. He always stays to make trouble."

"Romance is a beautiful thing," Pansy said.

"And there can never be too much of it," Helen agreed.

"I don't know if I can resist him," Liberty said, "if he's going to go all soft and gentle on me."

"Stick to the recipe," Helen advised. "It's working."

"And besides," Pansy said, "we want to conduct an experiment." She smiled innocently at Liberty. "We want you to spend a day in Duke's office with him." Holding up an imperious hand, she continued, "I know it doesn't sound exciting.

Heaven knows it may even sound dull as dish-water."

Liberty wondered if they understood just how tempted she was by Duke. This gown-down business was going to be harder than they thought if close proximity was suggested. "I have my bridal business to keep me busy," Liberty said. "I don't want to be in Duke's office. And I'm trying to decorate a nursery."

"We can help with that," Helen said, "but you need to spend a day walking in Duke's boots so you can appreciate him better. And vice versa."

"Vice versa?" Liberty asked.

"Oh, yes," Pansy said, "Duke needs to spend a day with you in your business, so he can better appreciate you! That's the assignment," she finished, satisfied.

"He'll never agree," Liberty said.

"Oh, he already has," Helen said. "He said being with you in your bridal boutique might be the closest he ever got to seeing you in a wedding gown."

Chapter Eleven

"I suppose," Liberty said the next day as she walked into Duke's office, "Swap Day is a good idea. It'll give me a chance to see what it's like to be the sheriff." She set a picnic basket down on Duke's desk. He stared up at her, completely surprised.

"Are you bringing me lunch?"

She gave him a soft smile. "How do you know I didn't just bring enough for myself?"

He grinned. "Sounds like you're softening."

"I'm not." She hung his hat on a hook by the door. "I'm bringing us lunch in case we have to work through the noon hour. Besides, I get hungry more often now."

His grin widened. "Eating for two."

"No, I'm eating just for myself, thank you. This is pound cake and there are sandwiches." She looked inside the basket. "Oh, and cottage cheese and vegetables for baby. You can share the vegetables if you like."

"No, thanks. I'll stick with cake." He propped his boots on the desk. "So what brings you in here?"

She looked at him. "You agreed to Swap Day, did you not?"

"In theory. I agreed to something. I'm not sure what the old gals pinned me to."

"If you don't want to do this—"

He grabbed her hand playfully, as if to keep her from escaping. "I'll do anything with you."

Liberty pulled her hand away. "Then you can't keep making remarks to Pansy and Helen or anyone like 'the closest you'll ever get to seeing me in a wedding gown is working at the shop with me.'" She slapped his hand lightly when he reached for her again. "Seriously, Duke. You get them all riled up. Swap Day wouldn't even have entered their heads if you didn't always say such things."

"Actually," Duke said, "I asked them for their advice."

"Oh?" Liberty put her hands on her hips. "On how to annoy me?"

"About how to make you happy," Duke said simply.

"I see," Liberty said. She was surprised and touched. "That's so sweet, Duke."

"That's me," he agreed, "the sweetest guy in Tulips."

She nodded. "Great. Now where do I start?"

He smiled in a wolfish sort of way. "Anywhere you'd like. The only things that are off-limits in here are the copper box in Mr. Parsons's cell—er, home—and my dog."

She laughed. "Your dog does as she pleases."

"Yes, so don't try to change her." Duke scratched his head. "Why is it that I have no pliable females in my life?"

"Because no one can be pliable around you, Duke," Liberty said tartly. "You're so hardheaded and stubborn and opinionated that a female just feels like she needs to stand up for herself or be taken completely over."

"Hmm," Duke said. "Okay. Maybe you can start your day by answering that ringing phone, please."

"Hello, Sheriff Duke's office," she said. "Yes, he's in." She handed him the phone.

"That's not the way to do it," he said. "Mr. Parsons asks who it is and what they want and then sometimes doesn't even give me the phone. He handles it himself."

"That's lazy," Liberty said. "Take your call."

He grunted. "Hello?"

Liberty watched him as he listened, thinking that he was handsome and kind in his own way, and a secret part of her was thrilled that she was having a baby with him.

"I have to make a run," he said after he'd hung up. "You don't want to make this one with me."

"Swap Day means we stick together." She tagged along behind him to the official sheriff's car. "We're going formal?" Duke usually drove his truck everywhere despite having a refurbished car donated by the town.

"For this one, yes. You could stay here and answer the phone—"

Liberty got in the car. "I could, but if anybody wants you, they know how to find you. That's if, and a big if at that." She gave him a sweet smile as he started the engine. "Besides, Swap Day is about learning to appreciate each other's worlds and getting to know each other better. How can I get to know you if I'm just answering your phone?"

He shrugged. "Don't say I didn't warn you."

"Actually, I didn't hear a warning."

"True," he said, "but it was implied."

"Oh," Liberty said, looking at Duke carefully—

was that a flush turning his brown skin somewhat ruddy? "Duke, where are we going?"

"To Flo Simmons's place," he said briskly, trying to sound nonchalant. Flo was the town man magnet, and Liberty hoped this run wasn't a common occurrence.

"This should be an interesting view into your world," Liberty said. "I'm so glad I'll have a front-row seat."

He gave a grunt that she deciphered as annoyance. *Smile and be of good cheer,* she remembered from the recipe, but it was hard when Duke was moody like this! "I can see why Pansy and Helen think your brother and sister might enjoy the sheriff seat more than you do," she said. "It seems to make you grumpy."

"It's not the job, it's the girl," he replied.

"Oh? Who?"

"You. You're determined to get under my skin today."

"Are you trying to tell me you didn't want me to come with you?" she asked. "This doesn't seem that exciting or dangerous to me."

He grunted again, and Liberty shrugged. "If grunting is your main mode of communication as a sheriff, no wonder everyone keeps away from you."

So he sighed instead. Liberty laughed. "I guess that's better."

They parked outside Flo's house.

"You could stay in the car," Duke said. "I'll only be a minute."

Liberty blinked. That was definitely a noninvitation. She watched Duke walk up the sidewalk, then decided there was no reason to sit in the car. They were supposed to be getting to know each other better and trying to understand each other's jobs. So she followed Duke to the porch.

The front door opened and Flo flew into Duke's arms, sobbing. Liberty blinked, smelling perfume and maybe some incense coming from inside the house.

"It's been so difficult, Duke!" Flo said. "Everything is just so hard on me these days!"

She was wearing a purple negligee, Liberty noted, so perhaps the only hard thing she wanted on her was Duke. "Excuse me," Liberty said. "Flo, you'd best put a bathrobe on."

"Liberty?" Flo detached herself from Duke. "What are you doing here?"

"Playing deputy," Liberty said, feeling Duke's gaze on her, "and if you don't get some clothes on, I'm going to be playing 'I Shot The Sheriff.'"

Embarrassed, Flo stepped back inside the house

and peeped around the door. All Liberty could see now was blond frazzled curls, red lips and a disappointed woman, which meant that was all Duke could see, too, and Liberty felt pretty good about it.

"I didn't know you were busy, Sheriff," Flo said. "Sorry for the trouble. Maybe I'll just handle my problem myself."

"Are you sure you're all right?" Duke asked, and Liberty gave him the slightest of pinches.

"I'm fine. Thank you. Thank you for coming out. Liberty, it's good to see you." She closed the door.

"Well," Liberty said, "I didn't realize your job was so *dangerous,* Sheriff." She headed down the walk and got into the car.

"Now, Liberty," he said, "I didn't know she was going to be dressed like that."

Liberty sniffed and looked out the window. "It's not worth discussing." She laid a hand on her stomach, feeling somewhat nauseated.

Duke didn't say anything else on the drive back, so neither did she. But Liberty realized that calls from lonely divorcées were part of his job. It wasn't his fault that he was a big handsome man whose job it was to be at the beck and call of the citizens of Tulips. She'd have to accept that, but it wasn't a cheering thought. Perhaps, selfishly, she couldn't help thinking about the fact that purple negligees weren't exactly part of her life right now, and might not be for a while. Women were going to throw themselves at Duke—after all, they lived in a town full of women who were single for one of a thousand reasons.

"How have you managed to stay single so long?" she asked, knowing she sounded disgruntled but not ashamed of it.

"You," he said. "I've always known there was only one Liberty who could set me free."

More pleased than she cared to admit, Liberty said, "You didn't look like you wanted to be free of Flo's arms."

He laughed. "Are you jealous?"

"Yes." She got out of the car when he parked and went inside the sheriff's office. "Hello, Mr. Parsons."

"Hi, Liberty." He was searching for something inside his cell. Duke came in and watched him for a moment, as did Liberty.

"Something wrong?" Duke asked.

"You didn't take the box, did you?" Mr. Parsons asked.

"No," Duke said, feeling slightly cold inside as he watched his elderly friend become more agitated. "It was there when we left. I'm positive of that because I told Liberty that was the one thing off-limits to anyone in here besides my floozie of a dog."

Mr. Parsons straightened. "It's gone." His face was a mask of worry. "The sheriff trusted me with that, and I let it get taken."

Duke resisted the urge to say that he'd suggested a more secure place for the town's documents. Sympathy held his opinion back on that. "Who would be interested in it?"

Mr. Parsons shrugged. "Could be anyone, I guess."

Liberty shook her head. "Even I didn't know the box was important until today. I'm sure it will turn up. I should probably go," she said to Duke.

"Wait," Duke said, following her out. "I detect a chill on this fine September day."

"No," Liberty said, "but it's clear from your last call that your job isn't that difficult. I think I've seen enough to appreciate it."

"Pacifying depressed townspeople is very difficult," Duke said, walking beside her. Liberty wasn't getting away from him in a temper in order to stew over something that had not happened— would never have happened—with Flo. He caught enough trouble for things that he'd actually done.

"And if some handsome man wraps me in his embrace and tells me how terrible life is—"

"I'll think he's a pathetic weasel," Duke said, "and I'll question your choice of friends."

She stopped to stare up at him. "Duke, it can't always be your way. I have feelings, too."

He kissed her hand. "Your feelings are my feelings."

"Not really." When she tried to take her hand away from his, he pulled her close and kissed her gently on the lips. That kept her retreat from happening, and Duke wondered if he had grabbed her at the altar and laid one on her if this whole dilemma could have been avoided.

"Your problem is not that you don't spend enough time with me," he said against her mouth, "but that we don't spend enough quality time together. In bed, where time counts."

"Yeesh," Liberty said, pulling away. "If you were talking to a less suspicious woman my dress would already be off." She headed toward her house.

"I like the sound of that," Duke said. "Let's see if we can detach you from your dress. My efficiency has never been questioned in that regard."

Liberty shook her head. "Pansy and Helen specifically instructed me to keep my clothing on around you."

He took her keys from her to open the door. "And I thought they were my friends."

"What are you doing?" Liberty asked as he walked inside with her. "You're supposed to understand that you're in the doghouse with me. And what about poor Mr. Parsons's box? You should be back there helping him find it!"

"He'll find it," Duke said. "No one's ever known what's in that box and I doubt we'll miss it now. I'm supposed to be having Swap Day with you, and that means it's now my turn to enjoy your job. I'm really looking forward to all these women in white."

Liberty frowned at him. "I vote we end Swap Day. It hasn't been a rousing success."

"Oh, it has," Duke said, sitting on the couch and pulling her down into his lap. "It made you appreciate me. That was the purpose of Swap Day, wasn't it?"

Liberty gasped as he undid her dress. "Duke!"

"Just checking to make certain your zipper is well-oiled."

She removed his hand from her bodice. "You really are a caveman."

"I'm a renaissance man, I swear," he said. "Let me see my baby. I've been dying to ever since I found out I was having one."

"That would involve taking off my dress."

"Precisely," he said, snuggling against her neck and moving his hand to her stomach, which he cradled possessively. "Let's break the code of chastity the old girls had you take. I want to see my child." He felt her shiver and knew he had her. "I've missed holding you, Liberty."

"Where do you think the box is?" Liberty asked. "Who would have taken it?"

Duke sighed. "Are you reminding me of my job on purpose?"

"Yes," Liberty said, her voice determined. "I am not falling for your tricks."

"Tricks!" Duke exclaimed, somewhat hurt. "Those were sincere statements of my feelings."

"I've just seen you in the arms of a purple-negligeed woman, and while it may have been innocent on your part, I'm going to need some time to digest," Liberty said stubbornly. "You're rushing me because of the baby, Duke. It's as if you're on a timetable you want me to fit."

He was. He'd vowed to have her at the altar before the baby came. His goal was marked for one week hence. "I'm not rushing things," he said. "I think we belong together for the sake of the child."

"I have to leave," she said. "I have an appointment in town."

"Great. I'll drive you."

She looked at him. "I don't like Swap Day."

"When you marry me, Liberty Wentworth, you'll know everything about me. Think about that. I know very little about you."

They stared at each other for a moment.

"I don't know where you went. I never knew much about your parents except that they neglected you. You're as much a mystery to me as my dog and Mr. Parsons's box, and if you think about it, I'm taking you on faith. You know the worst thing you're ever going to know about me is that women in nighties give me the occasional phone call for emotional support. And I never, ever, do anything more than listen." He grinned. "Actually, that only happened today, but I thought it made me sound sympathetic and big-brotherly."

"Not hardly," Liberty said. "My schedule is extremely tight today. Some brides-to-be are coming over from Union Junction on to look at gowns. You'll be bored stiff at the salon."

"I promise I won't be," Duke said. "I'll be with you, and that couldn't possibly be boring."

THREE HOURS LATER, Duke was bored out of his skull. He was also a little frightened. So much white! So many gowns, hanging everywhere like sparkly ghosts. It was almost eerie. He could swear he was breaking out in hives.

He didn't know how Liberty could take living in a world devoid of color and warmth. Right now, as he hid in a chair behind the cash register, he'd give anything for a nice, scratchy, colorful blanket of wool plaid to ward off the satin spirits surrounding him.

When they got married, Liberty was going to wear decent attire, he vowed to himself. Something with color in it that didn't make her look as if she were wearing a corpse's sheet. "I can't take this," he told Liberty. "I think I'm claustrophobic."

She laughed. "This shop is no worse than your grey, dank office."

"Have sex with me," he said. "I think I'd relax then."

A matron and her daughter glanced over at Liberty and Duke. "Sorry," Duke said. "Wedding jitters."

The matron smiled and the daughter giggled but he could tell Liberty was getting annoyed with him. Duke pulled his hat over his eyes and told himself to go to sleep.

The bell tinkled and more customers came in. He tried to shrink farther down into his hide-out post so he'd be less likely to hear any of what was going on. All of this bridal planning was making his skin itch.

"We just never seem to agree on anything," a bride-to-be told her friend. From under his hat, Duke watched the newcomers sift through the wedding gowns in a somewhat unenthusiastic fashion. "George and I don't always get along," she continued. "In fact, we rarely want the same things."

Her gaze lit on Duke and she smiled. He pushed his hat back and shook his head. "Don't do it," he whispered.

"Don't do what?" the almost-bride whispered back.

"Don't marry someone if you don't share the same goals. Goals are important."

She looked at her friend, who shrugged. ·

"But George is sweet," she told Duke.

"Sweet doesn't last thirty years. Enjoying each other and working toward the same things does." He looked around for Liberty and spied her coming toward them. Putting a finger on his lips so the bride would keep his secret, he pushed his hat back down on his head.

"You must be my three o'clock appointment," Liberty said warmly. "I'm Liberty Wentworth."

"I've changed my mind," the bride replied, sounding relieved. "I'm so sorry to waste your time."

"Changed your mind about a dress?" Liberty asked. "There are more gowns—"

"Changed my mind about my husband. Thanks, anyway, though. I'll be back when I find a man like him."

Duke cringed, knowing the bride had pointed to him. Liberty was going to believe the worst, of course. At the same time, his vanity was stroked. A man like him! The bridal business wasn't so different from his job, then—lots of advice and empathy required.

He heard the door open and close. Liberty went back to helping the matron and her daughter and he'd nearly begun to snooze when the doorbell tinkled again. Curious to see some more of Liberty's clientele, he watched as a middle-aged woman approached the dress rack with her grandmother.

"This is pretty," the bride-to-be said.

"Yes," her grandmother agreed. "You'd look lovely in that."

"Francis's mother mentioned that at my age I should probably wear a suit."

"Why would you listen to her?" her grandmother asked.

"I'm worried about looking my age," the bride replied. "Oh, hello," she said, noticing Duke eavesdropping on their conversation. "Do you work here?"

"My…lady friend owns the shop," he said, "and I vote you wear what you like."

She smiled at him. "Do you think?"

"Yes, I think it's your wedding, and no one, including Francis's mother, matters. However," he added hastily, "it's probably best if your mother-in-law-to-be doesn't exert so much opinion in your affairs." Duke looked around for Liberty, feeling guilty for speaking up, and yet unable to keep himself quiet. "Not that I'm an expert on marriage or anything, to be honest."

"But he's right," the grandmother said. The bride-to-be reluctantly nodded.

Liberty came over at that moment and Duke quickly pulled his hat down low. No wonder Liberty had had doubts about their marriage! If she had to listen to these sad-sack stories of doubt every day, it was no wonder she'd viewed marriage with some fear.

When she had their baby, he vowed she was going to stay home. He didn't want her working, especially not in this depressing environment! "I've nearly gone off marriage myself," he muttered.

Liberty took the hat off his head and slapped him with it before popping it back in place. "Duke

Forrester, what did you say to my customer? She said she had some thinking to do and left, and told me to tell you thank you!"

"Oh, boy," Duke said. "Liberty, we've got to talk."

Chapter Twelve

"Boundaries are important," Duke said. "Maybe we should set some after your customer leaves."

Liberty glanced at the mother and daughter who'd been shopping in her store. "That girl is shopping for a veil. Try not to frighten her, please."

Duke craned his neck to see. "Well, I'll try, but I can't promise anything."

"Duke," Liberty said, "are you running off my customers on purpose?"

"No," Duke said earnestly. "But, Liberty, I don't think I'm keen on this salon of yours."

"I believe I warned you."

Duke waved a hand at her. "It's more than that."

"Could you be more specific?"

"I don't know," Duke said. "All the white is disturbing my thinking process. And I think it's disturbed yours, too."

"I happen to think these gowns are gorgeous. Owning this shop was my dream, and designing my own label a bigger dream." She put her hands on her hips, irritated with him. "Why don't you step next door and have a nice hot mug of coffee to calm your nerves? The evil witch of the wedding wardrobe won't follow you out, I promise."

"Now, Liberty, it's not that bad." Duke shook his head. "But after the baby is born, I'm thinking you shouldn't work."

For a moment, Liberty was speechless. "Duke Forrester, you chauvinistic dope, of course I'm going to work! This is my dream whether you like it or not. I bought my house specifically so that I could run my business and look after my baby. I'm sorry you're so narrow-minded, but I can't see how what I've planned isn't the best of both worlds for my son."

"Son?" Duke said. *"Son?"* he repeated.

She looked at him for a long moment. "Congratulations, Sheriff, you're having a baby boy."

A grin broke over Duke's face. Finally, Liberty smiled at him, enjoying his happiness and his pride. Something passed between them, something of the happiness they'd shared before everything had become so difficult. A wistful tug pulled at her heart.

"Of course, no son of mine is growing up in a bridal salon, playing with dresses and high heels. I hope you realize that, Liberty." He crossed his arms. "A boy needs to be on the Triple F ranch where he can learn to be a man."

Liberty sucked in a breath.

"Is this a good time?" the shopping mother asked. "Because we can go for lunch and then come back."

"It's a perfect time," Liberty said. "Duke, go."

He blinked. "Go?"

"Yes. You're upsetting my customers. They can't shop with a jackass in the room."

"Oh." He looked crestfallen, sending an apologetic glance toward the women. "I'm sorry, ladies. I believe I'll head next door and get some coffee."

They smiled at him and he departed with one last glance at Liberty. She didn't smile at him, too upset to bend. How could she love that man so much when he was such a fathead? How could they ever live under the same roof?

"Sorry about that," she told her customers, but the mother shook her head.

"It wasn't a problem for me," she said. "It was a good experience for my daughter to see that marriage doesn't always go smoothly."

"Mom, I know that," the daughter replied.

"Duke and I aren't married," Liberty said. "As a matter of fact, I'm pretty sure we'll never be altar-bound."

"He's pretty strong," the mother said, "but I think he means well. I was listening to him give marital advice to your customers, and to be honest, he's pretty smart for a man."

"Really?" Liberty raised her eyebrows. "*Smart* wasn't a word that came to my mind."

"We'll take this veil," the mother said with a smile. "I like your boyfriend. He'll tame after a while."

"I don't know," Liberty said.

"He will," she said. "He loves you."

Liberty looked at her.

The mother laughed. "Honey, no man sits in a bridal shop unless he's desperately in love. Trust me. This is not a place they can remotely enjoy. Now if there were some big-screen TVs showing football, and a stash of cold beer and salami, that might be different."

Liberty smiled. It was true, and she'd tried to warn Duke. She went to hang the veil for her customers. Swap Day had clearly not been a success, though, and the worst part of that was they didn't understand each other any better now than they had before.

But she had to admit she loved Duke even a little bit more for trying to fit his machismo into her world of white femininity. Although now that he had found out his world was going to include blue baby booties, no doubt he was going to become even more insistent that everything go Duke Forrester's way.

DUKE COULDN'T STOP grinning. He was having a son! He didn't need coffee to feel hopped-up—his whole body was singing with jubilation. He would have been delighted for a girl, too, but now that he knew the sex of his child, the coming baby felt real to him. *Alive.*

He couldn't wait for the birth.

He couldn't wait to marry Liberty. What was wrong with a woman who worked in a bride factory who didn't want to get married?

She came in a few minutes later, seeming somewhat calmer. "Are you ready to go?"

He got up and followed her out. "Are we still friends?"

She looked at him. "Friends?"

"Yeah. I thought that perhaps I detected annoyance."

"Slightly. But yes, we're still friends. Although you're not good for my bottom line. That's the last time you hang out in my store."

"If I remember correctly, you prefer to sell dreams," he said. "That's what you're all about. I think you should stick to the program, and skip the ladies who think a wedding is the ultimate goal. Nothing lasting about that."

She nodded. "But it's not my job to judge. I'd be the last person to know if a marriage is right or wrong for someone. Honestly. Half the women who come in my salon have jitters. They sound unhappy, but they're really only running through a catalog of pre-wedding nerves."

"I think it got to you," Duke said. "You heard so many other women run through their insecurities that you decided you'd best join the crowd. We were perfectly happy at one time, you know."

"But I couldn't tell if I was looking forward to the wedding, or the marriage," Liberty said.

"Ouch," Duke said. "I thought great sex counted for something."

"It did, but I already had that. You can't rest on your past accomplishments."

He stopped her. "Liberty, if you think a couple of quickies—regardless that they resulted in a child—is the best you're going to get from me, you're going to miss out on the good stuff."

"Really?" She gave him a pointed look. "Are you saying you didn't do your best before? It's not like you to give less than your best. Maybe I feel slighted."

He laughed as she pulled away from him and got in the truck. "Liberty, you're going to have to take a chance and try me. I'm taking Swap Day to a new level, and I'm moving my office into your home. From this day forward, you and I will both be working out of that wedding cake you call a home."

"HE'S DRIVING ME NUTS," Liberty told Pansy and Helen the next day when they came over to her house to survey the moving-in process. "Ever since he found out about the baby, he's developed an insane streak."

"He already knew about the baby," Pansy said.

"But he didn't know the sex. Now he does and that made it real to him. He gave me a list of baby boy names this morning, all straight from his family tree." Liberty sighed. Duke's desk took up an enormous amount of space in her parlor, which, thank heaven, was big enough to accommodate the few things he was bringing. His own telephone and line, his desk chair and his dog, though he said Molly would probably need a doggie door if she intended to continue her disloyal ways.

"You could always kick him out," Helen said. "Tell him Swap Day isn't supposed to be permanent. It was one day and nothing more."

"I don't know." Liberty went over to his desk, her arms crossed as she looked down at Duke's things. A curious chill came over her. "He says I'm going to need help with the baby. But when I pointed out that he was only two streets away, he said if I wouldn't go to the Triple F with the baby, then he would be here. A family belongs together, in his royal opinion."

Pansy giggled. "I suppose I don't expect anything less from Duke."

A soft smile touched Liberty's lips. "A big part of me admires his commitment to this baby."

"Pfft," Helen said. "His commitment is to you."

"I like it," Liberty said quietly. "At least I think I do."

"Well, you can always toss him out," Helen said, "and I suppose I'd best head over to Hiram's cell. He'll be shocked having the place to himself. In fact, it may be hard on the old fart."

"She's really going over to see what the odds are being set at," Pansy whispered.

"What odds?" Liberty asked.

"Probably how long you and Duke can stick it out under one roof," Pansy said, following her friend. "It's the favorite pastime of the men, their primary vice in this town. And Miss Helen does love to be in the thick of it."

"You tell them no betting on my family," Liberty said. "Wentworths are winners. We're tough."

And Forresters were tougher, no doubt. Zach, Pepper and Duke were all cut from sturdy rawhide. The very thought of that ornery, possessive, handsome sheriff taking up residence in her house was enough to give her a complete case of nerves almost as bad as the ones she'd had on her wedding day.

Yet her body was traitorously looking forward to the sheriff and his promises.

DUKE FELT PRETTY GOOD about weaseling his way into Liberty's house. The idea of working from her home was a stroke of brilliance. He got to spend time with her, and even his dog seemed to be settling into the new routine.

But he minded the recipe and didn't remotely try to seduce Liberty, though it was killing him not to. He sat at his desk as he did every day; he took calls on the private line he'd had installed, and watched the goal date on his calendar get closer and closer.

But I'm making progress—I can feel it. Helen

and Pansy were right. Patience is definitely a virtue. I think.

The doorbell rang. Duke waited for Liberty to answer it—no one who was looking for him would ring. They'd all learned to bang on the window behind his portion of the living room. But when the bell rang again and she didn't answer it, he did.

A young woman and her nervous mother stood outside. "Welcome to Liberty's Lace," he said magnanimously, trying to do better than he had before. He intended to be encouraging. No more running off Liberty's customers, although he certainly didn't regret any of the advice he'd parceled out.

"Are you her husband?" the younger woman asked.

"I'm Sheriff Forrester," he said proudly. "I take up office space here."

Liberty came up behind him and gave him a look that said *make yourself scarce.* So, tipping his hat to the ladies, Duke hustled back to his desk.

He was not about to do anything that would give Liberty cause to boot him from her residence. As far as he was concerned, he was in—and it was just the first step to getting all the way into her life.

He pretended to get very busy with some paperwork, while the ladies moved farther into the newly-partitioned "salon." The soft sounds of ladies chatting reached him, and Duke felt himself relaxing. After sharing work space with Mr. Parsons for so many years, maybe the bride thing wasn't so bad. Perhaps her other salon had been too small, Duke decided—or maybe he'd been too close to the action. He felt safe tucked up here in his private little office.

"Excuse me."

Duke swiveled his head. The younger of the women was now dressed in a gown that complemented her perfectly—damn, her groom was going to be lucky—and she wore a veil that gave her a sexy, yet subtle, shyness.

He felt his blood rush to his head. He didn't want to get involved in case he said something that might be offensive to the bride-to-be. "Yes?" he asked carefully.

"Sheriff, I need a man's opinion."

He put up his hands. "I do not give opinions. Absolutely not. I gave up opinions for all time."

The bride smiled. "Okay. If you were my bride-groom, would you be happy to see me walk down the aisle in this dress? Just a simple yes or no."

"Hell, yes," Duke said, feeling himself break out in a sweat.

The bride said, "Thank you," with a pleased smile and wafted away.

"That was close," Duke told Molly, who was lying under his desk. "Liberty can't blame anything that happens on me. At least I don't think she can."

The bride and her mother left five minutes later, and when Liberty wasn't looking, the bride mouthed, "Thank you," to Duke, who gave her a surreptitious thumbs-up.

"I don't know what you said to her," Liberty said, "but that was the easiest sale I've ever made."

"Oh?" Duke said, concentrating on keeping his eyes on his paperwork. "Don't think I said more than six words to the woman."

"Really?" Liberty said. "She said you helped her make up her mind."

Duke looked up. "Seemed like her mind was already made up when she came in the house. That's a bride who's ready to marry her man."

Liberty looked at him. "Whatever."

She went into the other room. Molly gave him a sympathetic woof and lay her head down on her paws.

"Precisely," Duke said, as the doorbell rang again.

This time Liberty answered it, letting in three women—triplets, Duke noticed.

"Oh, how quaint and romantic your new shop is, Liberty," one of the three said.

"Nice to see you have a sheriff on the premises," another commented.

"Yes, I feel so *safe*," the third said.

Duke could feel a flush run up the back of his neck as the women giggled.

Half an hour later, he was in the middle of a brainstorm about the growth of the town when he heard *swish, swish, swish* in front of his desk. Glancing up, he was thunderstruck to see the triplets be-satined and be-ribboned in white, white, and more white. *I'm going to get a sign for my desk that says I have no opinions,* Duke thought. "What can I do for you ladies?"

"We're having our weddings together," one said, "and we want a man's reaction to the three of us in our gowns. Do we look different enough, or is it just too much white at once?"

"Well," Duke said, giving them more thoughtful consideration, "the bodices are all different, the skirts are all different and the veils you chose are different. Actually, I think the overall presentation is very foxy." He grinned. "I think your men couldn't help but carry each of you off at once."

"We're going to take all three," they said in unison. The trio bestowed a grateful smile on Duke, who hurriedly went back to work, hoping he hadn't gotten himself in deep with Liberty. *Maybe if I install a six-foot office partition and make myself a cubicle I'll get some peace. This is worse than sharing a place with Hiram.*

They left, a giggling group of excited brides. Liberty gave him a delighted smile as she closed the door. "Those were my own creations," she told him happily. "They didn't want dresses from a catalogue. They specifically wanted Liberty's Lace. Whatever you said to them, thank you so much!"

She threw her arms around his neck and Duke sat quite still from shock, enjoying Liberty's closeness and her breasts pressed against him. "So I can stay?"

"You can stay another day," she said, "since you're not running my customers off anymore."

"I didn't run the others off," he protested, but it was true he'd made more of an effort to flatter the female side of the women who'd been here today. Liberty floated off, so Duke whipped out his "recipe."

A Simple Recipe For Winning Your Woman
   Step One: Be kind. Romantic. Gentle. Think of days gone by. Try whispering instead of yelling; old movies instead of sex.

"It really was that simple," he told Molly. "I can't believe it. I almost believe the old girls may have known what they were talking about."

He read further with some trepidation and some enthusiasm.

Step Two: Consider her needs before your own.

The doorbell rang again. Sighing, Duke realized he was going to have to plan his reading time around Liberty's calendar—from now on he'd peep at it to see when she had fittings and showings scheduled.

But when Liberty let the young cowboy in— what was his name? Damian?—Duke scowled. Two other men walked in with the young pup, along with Valentine from Union Junction. Duke put away his recipe and gave the group his full attention.

Liberty and Valentine embraced. "Liberty, this is Hawk and Jellyfish, and you remember Blaine," Valentine said. "Guys, that scowling sheriff is Duke Forrester."

Hawk and Jellyfish nodded at him. They sized each other up cautiously.

"I'm delighted to see you, Valentine!" Liberty said. "What brings you to town?"

"We brought some baked goods for this week at the saloon," Valentine said. "We dropped them off already. But we have a favor to ask of you."

Hawk and Jellyfish grinned at her, giving the pup a push. "He wants a wedding gown," Hawk said, and Duke knotted his forehead. "Little brother's getting married, and he wants to surprise his bride-to-be with a special gown and all the trimmings."

Now that's an idea, Duke thought. *Wish I'd thought of it first.*

Chapter Thirteen

Duke decided he didn't want to hang around this crowd anymore. "It's nice to meet you all," he said to the congregation in the parlor. "I wish you the best of luck with your wedding, son. But if everyone will excuse me, I have sheriff duties I must attend to."

Liberty raised an eyebrow at him, but nodded. Just as he walked out the door he ran into Hiram and Bug. "What is it?" he asked. "Bug, what the hell is going on?"

Hiram said, "Sheriff, you gotta come quick!"

On second thought, maybe he should turn back and enjoy his comfy new office. Did Valentine mention something about cookies? "Not now, fellows," he said.

"Sheriff, it's important," Bug said, fairly hopping up and down.

"All right." Duke got up, resigning himself to the fact that cookies were not in his dietary plans for the day. He peered back through the window and saw Liberty was busy showing the pup and his contingent her wares. "Guess I won't be missed."

Hiram and Bug nearly pulled his arms off dragging him next door. "Easy!" he said.

"Shh!" Hiram instructed. "You have to be quiet!"

Duke hesitated. "Why are we in Ms. Helen's rose bushes?"

"We're spying," Bug told him, "so use your eyes and not your mouth, Sheriff."

The two of them stood on tiptoe and looked into Helen's kitchen. "See that?" they said to Duke in an urgent whisper.

Great. This fell under the heading of many law bendings and breakings, but maybe there was a problem that a sheriff should know about. Maybe Helen needed him! Worried, he joined them on tiptoe to peer through her kitchen window.

In the center of her kitchen table lay a copper box. Mr. Parsons's prize possession. Blinking with surprise, Duke eased himself down onto his heels, then dragged both his friends away and down to his old office at the jail.

"All I need is to get caught being a Peeping

Tom," Duke complained. "What the hell were you two doing looking in windows?"

"We came to visit you," Hiram said, "and I glanced over my shoulder toward Ms. Helen's kitchen, and I saw something shiny. I thought maybe she'd baked a cake—and put it under glass—that I could invite myself over for, so I took a look." He shook his head. "Then I called Bug to ask him what to do. He said it couldn't possibly be the town box, so he came and peeked, and then we got you quick as a jig. We didn't mean to spy, not really, even though we've been practicing on it."

Duke's old chair was now at his new office, so he had no place to sit. *Too bad—this one's got my legs feeling weak.* "Why would Ms. Helen take the box?"

Hiram looked at him, worried out of his skin, Duke could tell. "There are secrets we all have that could affect the town. One of them is in there. Or was." Hiram sighed. "My guess is Helen has no intention of allowing anyone to learn her secret. And the only person who knows her secret is me." He looked anguished. "I'll probably get fed some arsenic in my pound cake one day, just when I least expect it!" he wailed. "I'll be chewing along, tasting the powdered sugar, thinking how good life is, and the next I know I'll be—"

"Stop," Duke said, "you're making yourself ill, and your jangled nerves will kill you faster than Ms. Helen could. Let's think this through." He took a deep breath. Technically, what Helen had done was an arrestable offense. Unlawful entry, theft of city property—he couldn't bear to think about it. "Why didn't she just take whatever was in there that she wants kept secret?"

"Because the box is locked," Hiram said, "and only I have the key. You don't think I'm stupid, do you?"

Duke grimaced. Once this was straightened out, he was going to take charge of the city papers. They were going in an enormous, fire-proof, double-locked filing cabinet.

His brother and sister walked in with equipment and furniture. "What the hell?" Duke asked.

"We've decided to spruce this place up," Pepper said. "Since the town elders decided to remove you, and since you've removed your person from the premises, effectively giving up your position, we thought it was time to brighten up this mole hole."

Hiram and Bug had the grace to look ashamed when Duke glanced their way.

Zach nodded. "Mr. Parsons," he said gently, "you'll need to find another residence within thirty days. This is town property and should be used for official business only."

Duke stood still, taken completely aback at this proclamation. He'd been ousted, and without an election! Hiram and Bug shuffled their boots and looked anywhere but at him. He didn't know what to say himself. It was true the town's elders had decided he should be replaced; even Pansy had mentioned that he needed to spend lots of time with Liberty and their new baby if he was going to properly cement their family.

But he didn't want to give up his job. He loved his job. *If I'd told Hiram he needed to vacate, he would have protested and closed his cell door on me.*

On the other hand, he did have the ranch to run. And he wasn't one to hang around if he wasn't wanted or needed.

Then again, it would be nice to shove the box problem off on his siblings.

Hiram started rolling up his bedroll and packing up his few possessions. Duke stared at him. "What are you doing?"

"Moving out," Hiram said.

"You can't put him out in the street," Duke told his brother and sister.

"It's all right," Hiram said. "A little discipline

around this town won't hurt anything. It will probably be beneficial."

"Yeah," Bug agreed, "we can't be the wild west forever. Change is good, you know."

"Discipline?" Duke repeated, somewhat hurt. "Are you suggesting all the time you people were fighting with me that you actually wanted discipline? That's…childish!"

"We don't want to be treated like children," Hiram told him. "We want the town in firm hands." He carried his things to the door. "Be sure to tell your brother and sister that they need to go retrieve the you-know-what. In an official capacity."

Hiram left and Bug followed him.

"I'd say put the plant stand there, Zach," Pepper said as she pointed to a space in front of the window. "That will brighten things up. I'll start with a fresh coat of paint. Yellow, I think, since this room is so dark."

Duke glanced at the dingy walls, grey and old and just the way he liked them. "Paint seems an unnecessary expense to the town."

"Duke," Pepper said softly, "you have a lot to do. Why don't you go do it?"

"Don't I have to be officially removed? Voted out of office?" If it wasn't for the box issue—and he really wasn't looking forward to cornering Helen on the severe list of charges she was facing—he'd be extremely upset about his job being swept right out from under him.

"Not in this town," Zach said. "Same as the job got given to us, I guess it can be taken from you. Cheer up. They'll probably change their mind as soon as we crack down on them. We have lots of ideas for changes."

"I hate change," Duke said. "I guess you know that."

Pepper laughed. "Yes, brother, we know all about that. It's one of the reasons we have your job. Fresh paint and fresh ideas is what's needed in this town." She gave her brother a hug. "Nothing lasts forever, you know."

"Yeah, but I really was doing more than just taking up space," Duke grumbled. "Say, if you're going to be the new sheriffs, there is a matter that requires your attention." He said this with some glee, happy not to have to be stern with his friend. "Ms. Helen stole the box of records, or at least we assume she stole it because it's sitting on her kitchen table."

"Box of records?" Pepper asked.

"Yes, we don't use file cabinets or safes or anything remotely resembling sensible order in this town," Duke said with some satisfaction because he wouldn't be the one having to clean up what he'd said all along needed to be done. "Be easy with her because she's a friend." He stretched, enjoying the fact that this time he didn't have to play the role of plot-buster. "Guess I'll head to Liberty's and then the ranch. Enjoy your new job, and congratulations."

"Wait a minute," Pepper said, "I'm not going over there and telling Ms. Helen she's broken several laws."

"Oh, yes, you are," Duke said, pinning his badge on her, "and I'm going to enjoy watching you try to do it."

"Her feelings are going to be hurt!" Pepper exclaimed.

"Why would she steal it?" Zach asked, obviously trying to be sensible.

"Because she's hiding something," Duke said. "That's my theory. But that's your problem now." With a grin, he scooped up Molly's dog bowl and headed back to Liberty's.

Of course, when he got there, everything was in disarray—should he have expected peace and quiet? "Who are all these people?" he asked Pansy, who was hovering near the front door with a batch of fresh-made cookies on a silver tray. Swiping a tulip-shaped cookie, he glanced around him. Even his desk wasn't immune to the crowd—it had been covered with a white tablecloth and a colorful, fragrant floral arrangement had been placed upon it.

"They've come to the grand opening of Liberty's Lace," Pansy said proudly. "Our girl is such a smart businesswoman! She's the next Vera Wang of wedding gowns, I do believe."

He was about to grumble that he couldn't work like this, then remembered he wasn't the sheriff any longer and, technically, his desk was being used in an appropriate way, all things considered. He spied Holt in the next room fixing a bride's hair and fitting a veil on her head. Now was probably an opportune time to follow "the recipe." "Is there anything I can do to help?"

"You can make certain that Hiram got moved in upstairs safely," Pansy told him.

"Hiram! What do you mean, *moved in upstairs?*"

"Well, he had to go somewhere since your siblings evicted him." Pansy shook her head. "Never thought I'd see the day a Forrester would evict anyone." She sighed. "However, he knew Liberty wouldn't turn him away, and since you were here, he figured this was a good place for him, too. He said two varmints were no more trouble than one. It was getting rid of them that was a pain, but he didn't figure she'd be wanting to get rid of him any more than you."

Duke didn't think of himself as a varmint. He frowned. "I don't think I will help Hiram since he was one of the ones who wanted me out of office."

Pansy patted his arm. "Now don't take that personally, too."

He sighed. "Wasn't the purpose of me having Swap Day with Liberty so that we could get to know each other?"

"Precisely," Pansy said, "and I suppose you did if you moved your office here."

"I should feel better," Duke said, "but all I can think of is that Liberty has lots of plans for everything but me."

"Duke, you knew she was an independent, smart girl," Pansy said with a smile. "She had it too hard growing up to simply think marrying a man would solve all her problems. That was the exact reason she left you. You expected to take care of her, and Liberty knew she had to take care of herself first or she'd never be truly secure."

"I never thought of it that way," Duke said. "I took it personally."

"I know you did," Pansy said, "and I'm not saying Liberty couldn't have handled the situation better. But all Liberty knew was she loved you like mad—until she was standing at that altar and realized she'd left one major ingredient out of the recipe of life. I have to say I admire her for making a difficult decision, even it did start tongues to wagging."

Duke took that in for a moment, seeing Liberty through a different type of glass.

"You know, Duke, probably the scariest part for Liberty was that she never knew if you could forgive her."

Forgive her? Had he? Now that he thought about it, maybe he had merely glossed over the bad feelings and resentment. No wonder nothing had been easy with Liberty. "I've been trying to fit this onto a timetable," he said. "Our relationship, everything. But now I see it's better not rushed."

"You're too right," Pansy said. "Traditional ideas versus modern ones, you know. Excuse me while I circulate. I'm Liberty's new assistant and receptionist, since her business is growing so fast, so I must do my job."

She moved away, taking the tray of cookies with her. A thieving elderly woman, disciplinarian siblings, a vagrant town elder moving into Duke's new domain and—he narrowed his gaze at Hawk and Jellyfish as they carried in bolts of fabric,

setting them in the room where Liberty direct-
ed—he wasn't sure what to think of those new
friends of Liberty's.

"Okay," he said, "I might as well go to the ranch
where there's no siblings and no wedding gowns.
Where's my dog?" He looked for Molly, finding
her perched on a box wearing a wedding garter for
a collar, enjoying herself thoroughly. "Great," he
said. "I'm leaving, floozie," he told her. She raised
a paw at him, and he left, recognizing the signal
for *not now, I'm busy being a ham.*

"I'm going to go find my life," he said to no one
in particular, heading off to think through what it
meant exactly to be a resident of Tulips without
his job and without his woman.

Chapter Fourteen

Three hours later the last guest had left, Hiram was tucked into a back room upstairs and Liberty had cleaned everything, including the white tablecloth off Duke's desk. She couldn't blame him if he'd been irritated when he'd come in and seen that. "Come on," she told Molly, "let's go find your master and see how he is coping with being a man of leisure."

The dog followed her to her truck and jumped in. They drove to Duke's house and got out. Liberty nearly rang the doorbell, then decided she, too, could be nontraditional. Picking up a handful of rocks, she tossed them at Duke's bedroom window, hoping he was in there.

She didn't have long to wait as the rocks flew through the glass. "Oops," Liberty said, "that never happens in movies."

"What the hell?" Duke yelled, lifting up a window that wasn't shattered. "Liberty Wentworth, you just broke my window!"

"I noticed," Liberty said. "Guess you could arrest me for breaking and entering."

He frowned down at her. "You haven't entered, so I can't."

"I'd like to," she said. "Sheriff."

She saw the ire fade from his face and reached down to pet Molly.

"All right," he said, "but you have to hold the window while I putty in a new one."

"Sounds like romance to me," Liberty said, and waited on the front porch for Duke to open the door.

"I won't say what I might have said yesterday," Duke said, opening the door so she and his dog could come in.

"Which is what?"

"That if we were married, you'd have a key to your own house," Duke said. "Come on up."

The three of them went upstairs.

"Why wouldn't you say that?" Liberty asked.

"Because I've changed."

She took the broom he handed her and began to sweep up the broken bits of glass. "Why?"

"Because I realized I was rushing to fit you into my timetable. And that maybe I was going too fast for all of us. Keep sweeping, I'm going to go get a pane of glass and the putty from the garage." He grinned at her. "Nice of you to drop by, Liberty, but next time, you can be more gentle about it."

He laughed at his own wit, since everyone was always telling him he was a bull-in-a-china-shop type of guy and she'd been the one who'd broken something.

"Yeah, I get it. Ha ha, hee hee," Liberty said. "Molly, your father will probably howl, but you get up on the bed so I can make sure you don't cut a paw on some glass."

A moment later, Duke was back. "What makes you need to see me so desperately that you break my window?"

Liberty scooped the glass into a nearby trash can. "I didn't get to talk to you today. I had this strange sensation that I missed you. Or it could have been heartburn. Sometimes I get that with the baby now."

"That's funny," Duke said. "I had heartburn, too."

"Do you still?"

"I don't know." Duke sighed. "Liberty, I'm trying really hard to figure everything out. What it means to be a father, what it means to be an ex-fiancé. I want you to be happy."

"I am," she said softly. "Duke, I've made a lot of mistakes."

Putting the putty and tools down, he looked at her. "Let's fix this later. I'd rather sit and talk to you right now."

"I'd rather you hold me," Liberty said. "I'm afraid I'm losing you."

If ever there was an invitation, Duke was positive that was it. He took Liberty in his arms before she could retreat on him again, and gave her the kiss he'd been wanting to give her on their wedding day that didn't happen. He took her mouth with his, kissing her lightly at first, letting her know she'd always be safe with him, then he deepened his kisses as if he could melt inside her.

"Let's make love, Duke," she said on a sigh.

He pulled back to look down into her eyes. "I'd hurt something."

She smiled. "Not if you're gentle."

"Oh, hell, I can be gentle," Duke said, "but Liberty, I think my son likes having you all to himself right now."

"He is possessive, but he's safely tucked away up under my rib cage." She tugged his shirt out of his pants.

"No, we're not doing this," Duke said, removing her hands. "I rushed us. I'm not going to rush the baby. I have the rest of my life to make love to you, even if you won't do it wearing white."

"I'm going to wear white one day," Liberty said.

"I've changed my mind about that."

Liberty looked at him. "Changed your mind?"

"White is no longer my favorite color. I want you in red when you say, 'I do.' Hot, hot red. Tulips red."

She put her head against his chest. "If you make love to me, I'm positive I'll be able to remember feeling like a woman who wears hot, hot red."

He stroked her hair—it was one of his favorite sensations in the world and one he'd missed the most. "You are an incredible woman."

"So?" Liberty asked, and he heard the question in her voice.

"What about keeping your gown down?"

"They don't know everything," Liberty said with a giggle. "It was only the first ingredient of the recipe, anyway. We should try making our own."

"You've talked me into it," Duke said, unzipping her dress. "I can't wait another minute to hold you, so if something hurts—"

"It won't," Liberty said, pulling at his jeans. "Quit talking, Duke. I swear that's all anybody in this town does."

"Off the bed, floozie," Duke commanded in a tone even the dog knew to obey as she vacated the room. He closed the door, locked it and picked Liberty up to slide her onto his bed. "Finally, I've got you all to myself."

Carefully, he eased her dress from her, gasping as he saw her stomach. Liberty tried to hide it, but Duke pushed the sheet away. "Is that my son?" he asked in amazement. "Look at the size of him! You sure have grown in the last couple of weeks."

"Duke," Liberty said, trying to cover herself, but he wouldn't let her, and leaned in to rest his head against her stomach.

"He's nice and warm," he murmured. "There's probably no place my son would be happier than inside you. He may never come out."

Liberty laughed, a nervous sound. Duke realized she was uncomfortable and pulled the sheet up for her. "You're beautiful pregnant," Duke said. "I had no idea pregnancy was such a sexy thing."

"Do you really think so? I feel like a basketball is lodged inside me."

"By God, if you do, it's a winning team," Duke said. "I can't wait to autograph it." He climbed up into the bed, taking the rest of her clothes from her in a rush of heat. "Liberty Wentworth, I have never gotten over you leaving me." He kissed her neck, then her breasts, slowly, lovingly, enjoying Liberty's sighs of happiness. Then he kissed every inch of her belly, glorying in the changes he'd made in her body. "I'm so glad I got to experience this," Duke whispered. "Thank you for coming back to Tulips. I would have missed the best part of my life if you hadn't."

She pulled him inside her, greedy to feel him, touch him and hold him close. Liberty closed her eyes. Nothing felt this good—not satin, not silk, not velvet. Duke Forrester was the only man she could ever love, and she loved making him happy. "Everything feels different," she murmured. "Even better than before."

"I'll just keep you pregnant, then," Duke said, stroking his lips against hers. Liberty smiled, putting her hands along his face to hold him close to her, her heart beating hard.

"When I was growing up," she said, "I thought you had the perfect family. I always wanted to be part of it."

"Now that you're grown-up," Duke said, moving deeper inside her, "you'll find out we are far from the perfect family. But you can definitely make us better."

Liberty closed her eyes, her heart warming and a climax taking over her as Duke's hands worked their magic all over her body. She felt safe, secure and ecstatic as she cried out her pleasure, and when Duke captured her lips with his, she felt passion that she'd never known sweep her away, like nothing could ever hurt her again.

LIBERTY SLEPT in Duke's arms, not waking until about two o'clock in the morning. She hated to leave—she'd slept more soundly these past few hours than she'd slept in months. But she didn't want to run into Zach and Pepper in the morning, and she didn't want all of Tulips to know she hadn't been home—which they would with Hiram living upstairs and Pansy and Helen living next door.

So she crept out of bed, leaving Duke alone in an empty bed in a room with a broken window. *Good thing it's a mild September.* She grinned, not regretting that she'd done that at all since she'd ended up in his bed. In fact, she didn't regret anything about tonight.

Downstairs, she quietly fed Molly, and then went to her truck. Backing out of the drive, Liberty looked at the Forrester homestead, nearly crying tears of joy that she, too, was becoming part of a family that loved her.

When she pulled into her own drive, she saw

someone crossing the street, heading due north toward the town square. Liberty hesitated, realizing it looked an awful lot like Helen. Maybe something was wrong! She parked her truck in the drive and followed her friend, curious.

Helen went inside Duke's old sheriff's office. Liberty watched as a light went on for just a second, then went off. A few moments later, Helen walked out, heading for her own house. Liberty couldn't stand it a second longer.

"Helen," she said, and the older woman screamed, nearly jumping out of her heels.

"Liberty! You nearly gave me a heart attack!" Helen glanced around, then lowered her voice. "Why aren't you in bed?"

"I…I wasn't sleepy yet," Liberty hedged. "Why are you taking such a late-night stroll?"

"I couldn't go to sleep," Helen said, "and then I decided a walk might help, and then I went looking for Hiram. But then I remembered he's staying at your place now," she said brightly. "Silly me."

"It's not going to work," Liberty said softly. "I saw you carrying the box."

"Oh," Helen said. "Box?"

"The box with the town records inside."

"Well," Helen said with a sigh. "Come on over to my house. I think we should talk."

"It's late," Liberty said. "Can't it wait until to-morrow?"

"I might be dead tomorrow," Helen said briskly, "and I'd rather explain my actions than have people try to figure them out after I'm gone."

"All right." Liberty walked with her old friend to her house, and Helen unlocked the door. Once inside, she smelled the comforting fragrance of a clean home.

They sat at the kitchen table together, no tea, no cookies this time. Helen looked at her for a long time, as if she were trying to decide what to do. Her hands trembling, she took out a piece of paper, holding it in front of her.

"A long time ago, Liberty, when you were just a little girl—sort of a motley, maybe even mischie-vous little girl, but we all loved you—we didn't understand why your parents didn't take better care of you. I can tell you that we were all relieved when the Forresters took you in. That was after your parents left, of course."

Liberty sat still. Even now the feelings of resent-ment and desertion stung her harder than she would have thought they still could. "I don't think much about that anymore," she said, wanting it to be true.

"Well." Helen nodded. "I wouldn't want to,

either. However, when you were left here, you weren't exactly left." She put the paper on the table between them. "I stole this from the box. It's adoption papers, for you."

Liberty stared at the paper. Her hand trembling, she reached out to pick it up, her eyes reading words blindingly fast, as facts mixed with emotions that had pain barbed all through them. "You adopted me," she murmured. "Helen Granger agreed to…" She stopped, nearly speechless until she could make her mouth move. "Why?"

"Mrs. Forrester agreed to take you in if I would be your guardian and adopt you. Duke's mother felt it would be best if there were two of us looking out for you. I'd never had a child, so then I had you." Helen's mouth worked for a moment before she said, "Mrs. Forrester felt that in case your parents ever came back for you, there'd be two of us to fight in a custody battle. Duke's mother had the money, and I had the power in the town. We felt pretty good about your future at that point. Between us, we felt we could give you a chance." She watched to see how Liberty was taking this information. After a moment, she said, "We felt you'd been abandoned enough. You deserved better. Maybe we could have come up with a better plan, but this was many years ago." She touched Liberty's hand. "I would do it all over again just the same."

"Who knows this?" Liberty asked.

"Not a soul, except perhaps Hiram, though his mouth is as secure as a locked box. That's why I went to steal these papers. I didn't want anything in a place where Duke…or you, or his siblings, might find out the truth. The time has passed for it to matter, after all."

Liberty felt tears jump into her eyes. "It feels weird. I suppose I should say thank you."

Helen shook her head. "No. I thank you. You've been an angelic daughter. And now I'm a grandmother, something I would have never been without you."

They looked at each other over the table. Liberty fought back tears and emotions that were sharpened by her pregnancy hormones, but it was nearly impossible. "Did my mother say why?"

Helen sighed. "Liberty, your parents…were different sorts. They didn't really fit in here, didn't make an effort. They weren't cut out to be parents. They didn't work. I don't mean to criticize, but they were a bit odd. They had their own ideas of how things should be. Now, we're all pretty stubborn around here and we do have our battles, but we love each other and take care of each other." She shook her head. "That wasn't their way. One day, they just decided to get in their old car and drive off. And no one's heard from them since. Of course, it had nothing at all to do with you, and I suspect if not for you, they would have never had any stability at all."

Liberty shook her head. "I always thought I was in their way."

"Honey, they were in their own way. That's all there was to it." Helen took her fingers between her own. "Mrs. Forrester and I loved you, Liberty, and we were so grateful to watch you grow up. You have no idea how many happy hours we spent at this very table discussing your future. Talking about how you were the sweetest, most beautiful girl in town. Mrs. Forrester was just as proud of you as her own children." She smiled. "She'd be happy about you and Duke."

Liberty tried to smile, too. "I thought that myself the other day. But why didn't you tell me?"

Helen sighed. "I don't think I ever foresaw the day I would tell you. You were so beautiful and happy, or at least you seemed so to us. We just wanted you to stay that way."

Liberty thought about Duke and how she hadn't married him because she didn't feel that she was ready at the time. She had known she wasn't fully developed as a woman, and Duke was so strong…this piece of information filled in the gaps but saddened her as well. "I didn't understand my parents. I hope my children understand me."

"They'll understand that you love them," Helen said, "and their father, too."

Liberty smiled, already missing Duke and the strength he brought into her life. "It's okay now," she said. "I'm not worried about a thing."

"Good," Helen said, "that's the way we wanted you to be." She smiled. "You're not angry with me?"

"No," Liberty said, "although this town has got to quit keeping secrets."

"I don't think that's possible," Helen said, "but I couldn't say for sure."

Liberty gave her a mock-stern gaze. "We have got to get our act together in this town."

"Too true," Helen agreed, "and we're starting with you."

Chapter Fifteen

Liberty went home, thinking about how much her life had changed, and still happy that she and Duke were becoming much closer, but her pleasant thoughts were suddenly interrupted by a blinding pain.

Sweat broke out above her lip. Gasping, she sat down, clutching her abdomen. She felt water break and more pain than she'd ever known and realized she would soon be face-to-face with her past, present and future.

"Mr. Parsons!" she exclaimed, and an upstairs door opened immediately.

"Liberty? Did you call me?"

She gasped, holding her stomach. Mr. Parsons didn't drive, nor did Helen or Pansy. "Could you please call Duke?"

"Duke? At this hour?"

"Yes, please," Liberty said.

"What shall I say to him?" She could hear his footsteps on the stairs.

"That I think it's time," Liberty said on a groan.

Mr. Parsons peered from his spot on the stairs at her, assessing the situation correctly because he didn't say another word as he dashed back up to his room. Liberty leaned her head back and waited for the pain to pass.

Twenty minutes later her front door crashed open. Duke stood in the doorway, a true cowboy riding to the rescue.

"Do you have to be so dramatic?" she asked weakly.

"Liberty!" Duke exclaimed. "Are you all right?"

"I'm sort of fine," she said to calm him down, "but I'd like to go to the hospital."

He checked his watch. "You're too soon," he said, "and we're not married."

Trust Duke to fall back on the order of life as he planned it. "Do you want to deliver this baby?"

"No," Duke said, "but I'll be with you every second." Scooping her in his arms, with a worried Mr. Parsons holding the front door open, Duke carried Liberty to his truck. "It's not as comfortable as an ambulance."

"It's better," Liberty said, trying to ward off the pain. "I trust your driving."

"Damn it, can I get a seat belt on you?" Duke let the seat belt fall back into place. "Never mind. You just lie back there and I'll drive like a taxi driver."

"Great," Liberty said, "and I'll be sick like a tourist." She put her head down on the cab's back seat and tried to relax between cramps, really not feeling like teasing anymore, even though she was trying to keep Duke from being so worried.

Not a half hour later, he pulled into the emergency drive at the hospital in Dallas, hopping out to help her to the curb and then inside to the counter. "We shouldn't have made love," he grumbled.

"That's a fine excuse," Liberty said. "But shut up for now while I pant. And unattractively grunt."

"Nurse," Duke said, speaking to an orderly who was walking by.

"Over there, Dad," the orderly said, pointing to the check-in counter.

"This isn't going to be as easy as it looks." Duke seated Liberty in a chair. "You wait there, and I'll check us in."

Liberty was in too much pain to question Duke's plan. "I'm not going anywhere."

She was sooner than she thought she was, because someone apparently ordered her to be helped from the chair to a gurney, and from there she was wheeled into a room and completely checked over. Liberty answered questions as coherently as possible, until she realized that she was going into surgery.

Then she got scared. "What's wrong?" she asked Duke, who clung to her bed rail and stared down at her.

"Nothing," he said, "except our baby is impatient. Takes after his dad, I'm sure. Impatient is my middle name." He tried to grin at Liberty, but she could tell he was shaken. "Hey," he said. "I love you."

"Well," she said, closing her eyes, "hold that thought until I get out, okay?"

He kissed her forehead. "You can hold that thought forever," he said. "It's not going to change."

Liberty had something to say, something pertinent she was certain, but the baby really was an impatient Forrester, and suddenly she was occupied with the business of becoming a mother.

DUKE COULD BARELY contain himself, but when he was finally ushered in to see his newborn son, he couldn't take his eyes off him. "Wow," he said proudly, gazing down into the bassinet. "Look at this little man!"

He wasn't certain if the tubes in the baby were normal, but Liberty smiled at him so he relaxed. "You're beautiful," he said.

"Thank you."

"Of course, you know the baby is beautiful," Duke said. "He looks just like me."

Liberty didn't laugh or shoot back a comment, so Duke knew she was probably in pain. "Was it very hard to give birth?" He held her hand and sat on the edge of the bed to be close to her.

"The doctor said everything was normal, but yeah, it hurt! I just wish I could have gone full-term. I feel as if I cheated our son."

"Oh, he looks healthy enough." Duke brushed her hair out of her eyes. "Let's make another one right now."

Liberty held her stomach and tried not to laugh. "I'm going to sleep now."

"You do that," he said softly, touching her face. "You're amazing," he said even more quietly, meaning every word of it. "I love my baby. And I love you, too."

Liberty's eyes had drifted shut. "Call Helen, and tell her she has a new grandson to enjoy."

Duke smiled. "Drugs getting to you, baby?"

"No," Liberty said. "Helen had the box."

The smile left Duke's face. "*The* box?"

"Yes. She didn't want anyone to know that she'd adopted me many years ago. But, strangely, I feel all the more loved because of what she and your mom did. I feel like all the gaps in me are filled in. Please don't arrest Helen for stealing the box, Duke."

Liberty's voice sounded so tired that Duke began to worry. "Are you okay, my little tulip?"

Liberty opened her eyes. "I feel stronger because of you. Don't forget to call Helen. She'll be worried."

Come to think of it, he had a ton of people he'd better call. They'd all want to bring presents and baked goods. "So did she put the box back?"

"Yes."

"And whatever she…removed?" He didn't want to say *stole* about the new grandmother of his son.

"It was on her kitchen table."

Duke shook his head. "I'm glad I'm not sheriff anymore, unofficially speaking, of course, but just the same. Gives me plenty of time to enjoy my new family." He softly touched Liberty's nose. "We have some decisions to make."

"I know. Like the baby's name."

Duke nodded. "I was thinking Michael Zachariah, even though my brother took over my office."

Liberty smiled. "I like it. And don't worry about your office. I have a plan."

"No plans for you, lady." He kissed her and then went to sleep in the hard chair nearby, a content grin on his face. "No plans for a long time in the Forrester family."

Forrester family. It sounded so good. So permanent.

I finally caught her.

Two weeks later, in her little house on Pear Street, Liberty knew she had to make some changes. The baby had finally come home in fine health, and she was recovering nicely, thoroughly in love with little Mikey, as Duke called him. Mr. Parsons tried to stay out of the way upstairs, making himself busy by doing laundry and keeping groceries in the house. Every day there was something cooking in the Crock-Pot. Mr. Parsons had bought a book on Crock-Pot cooking, saying he had to earn his keep, he'd never had to cook before and was enjoying learning how. He intended to cook in the oven in the near future.

Duke kept his desk downstairs, which somehow had become a baby-present holder, but he didn't seem to mind. What he did mind, Liberty knew, was her tiny little house. He felt cramped. And customers still needed their fittings, which Pansy and Helen had taken over for her, but it still meant brides and family members in the house.

All the company meant no time for the three of them to bond as a family.

So even though it was easier for everyone to visit her at the little white house, and even though Helen and Pansy would be disappointed that the baby wasn't right next door, Liberty had Duke help her pack up and move their family to his house.

He liked that, she knew. He could tend to his chores now, and she could often hear him whistling. Not once did he ever mention his sheriff's office on Main Street, seeming content to let Pepper and Zach run things in their unofficial capacity.

Liberty was pretty certain Duke was as happy as she'd ever seen him. And so was she. Not really knowing what to expect of having a baby, she was surprised by how in love with him she was from the instant he was put in her arms.

It made her love for Duke deeper and more resonant than ever before, and that was saying something considering she'd loved him all her life.

Duke walked in, grinning at her. "You're sexy in the morning."

She raised a brow at him. "So are you."

"I can't wait for the doctor to give you the all-clear."

A smile touched her lips. "But I think I can make you happy until then."

His attention riveted to her. "Did I ever tell you I like it when you stroke my ego like that?"

She laughed. "I think I could figure that out on my own."

"I knew I picked a smart woman." He put on his bolo tie. "Can you make it without me for a couple of hours?"

"Well, yes and no," Liberty said. "I can, but I'd rather have you with me."

He nodded. "Little Mikey Zach said he'd keep you busy until I came home. All seven pounds of him—think he can take my place for a while?" He came over and gave her a lingering kiss. "Pepper and Zach said they needed some help in my office."

"Your office?" She smiled at him.

"Hell, yes. I'm just letting those squatters think they know what they're doing. They have no clue what they're getting into with the town elders, and I believe my siblings are just beginning to figure out that they are hand-picked stool pigeons for the Tulips Saloon Gang."

Liberty smiled. "There really is no Tulips Saloon Gang."

"Ha!" Duke stroked her hair. "I've got one of the foremost gang members in my bed right now."

She rolled her eyes. "I never realized what an imaginative sort you are."

"When I come home, I plan on being really imaginative with you, so be prepared."

That sounded very good. "I hope you're a man who keeps your promises."

"Although," he said, his forehead wrinkling, "I was reading a baby book, and it said that sometimes women get touched-out when they have a newborn. Like, it's all overload and they'd really rather have a bath than—"

"No," she said definitively. "Touch me all you want, Duke Forrester, and throw out that book. I don't think we need any more tips from anyone."

Mikey Zach let out a wail. Duke grinned. "Takes after his father, I'm proud to say."

"Yes," Liberty said, "it's all his way or no way."

"All men like to be spoiled," he said happily. "You girls and your recipes for love ought to figure that out at some point." He left, whistling happily.

Liberty gasped. The recipe! She'd forgotten

all about the recipe on *Romancing Your Stubborn Sheriff*.

She didn't think she needed a recipe anymore. She felt pretty certain she'd figured out the key ingredients on her own.

So without any regrets, she fed her baby, and then began to pack a bag.

Chapter Sixteen

Duke walked into his old sheriff's office, noting the congregation already assembled: Pansy, Helen, Mr. Parsons, Bug, Holt and his own siblings. Every countenance carried a frown, and every posture was wired for dispute. "Hello, friends and family," he said jovially, then stared at his office with dismay.

"Duke," Zach began, "we only made a few adjustments."

"Certainly needed adjustments," Pepper said.

Duke grimaced at the yellow paint, the pretty flower pots in a stand and ribbons twined around Mr. Parsons's jail-cell door. "This is not a florist shop. This is a town office. It should look like one."

"Yes, we're just a little town called Depressing," Pepper said. "Come on, Duke. You know this place needed a pick-me-up."

He sighed. "So what's the first order of business?"

"We have some plans," Zach said, "and we're meeting fierce resistance."

"Oh?" Duke said, mentally rubbing his hands with glee.

"Yes. Some of our town members are overly opinionated." He glared across the room at the elders, and they glared back.

"You don't say," Duke chuckled.

"So we wanted to get your advice on how to proceed. There has to be a way."

"There's not," Duke said. "It's their way or no way. Though you could always ignore that and cause yourself real problems. What did you have in mind?"

"Well," Zach said carefully, "we don't really need a tearoom in this town. The Tulips Saloon building could be put to better use."

"Yes, we do," Duke said, earning a delighted smile from Helen and Pansy. "I used to think we didn't, but now I see how important saloons are to our way of life in Tulips. It's *commerce.*"

"There are no customers except us," Pepper said, but Duke shook his head.

"With Liberty's bridal salon opening, there has been a marked increase in the number of customers to the saloon. I know, because I see Valentine and her buddies here all the time delivering baked goods." He frowned, thinking of Hawk and Jellyfish. "I'm surprised some of our good ladies haven't picked off some of those cookie-carriers Valentine always seems to tote with her. For example, you, sister."

Pepper gasped. "Oh, no. Not me, Duke. I'm not looking for a Hawk or a Jellyfish in my life."

Duke glanced at Holt. "Holt, you've cut all our hair for years. What do you think about the tearoom?"

"I think I'd like to stay out of the conversation," Holt said diplomatically. "I'm only here because it's time for Ms. Pansy's rinse. But she said she couldn't skip this meeting."

"Look," Zach said, "Duke, we propose an elementary school should be erected where the Tulips Saloon stands."

Duke stared at his brother in silence for so long that people in the room began shifting nervously. "Brother, have you lost your mind?" Duke finally said.

"Education before cookies," Zach said stubbornly.

Pepper added, "Education is important to the welfare of a town, Duke."

Pepper knew wherefore she spoke—she'd

chased education all her life. Frowning, Duke glanced at Pansy and Helen, gauging their reaction. "No," Duke said. "No town has an elementary school in the town square."

"They have courthouses. Why not a school? It's perfect for that big, old, basically empty space."

Pansy and Helen glared at Zach. "I think I'm sorry I wrote you in as sheriff," Pansy said. "I want Duke back."

"Me, too," Helen said. "He understands our foibles."

Duke's chest poked out about a foot. Now his townspeople were appreciating him!

Liberty rolled a white wicker bassinet into the office, startling everyone. "Hi," she said. "Can someone help me carry in the diaper bag and box of necessaries?"

"Liberty Wentworth!" Helen exclaimed. "What are you doing out of bed?"

"I haven't been in bed for days," Liberty said. "And besides, all of you are here. I might as well be, too." She smiled at Duke. "We're taking back our office."

"Can we do that?" Duke asked.

"Sure. If all we need to do is be on the premises, that's easy." She held the baby gently, cradling him against any chill. "I like the yellow, but the motif is going to have to be more plaid. Duke likes plaid, and I think his son does, too."

"As a doctor, I think—" Pepper began.

"As a mother, I think we should stand behind our man," Liberty interrupted. "Trust me, we'll all be happier this way."

"But what about the school?" Zach asked. "And the other reforms I want to implement?"

"Well," Pansy said, "I don't think we want that much reform."

"But Duke doesn't do anything," he said. "At least I want to make some positive change. That's my platform," Zach said.

"And change is good," Helen said, "but we like our sheriff doing nothing. He's usually doing nothing for us, and that's better than doing a lot of something we don't want."

Zach looked sad. "I really think a school would bring residents—"

"I couldn't agree more," Duke said. "We do need a new school. We just don't need to give up the Tulips Saloon. It's the heart of the town."

Pansy and Helen stood straighter, and Duke knew he'd never run short of baked goods on his plate in the future. Liberty handed him his son, whom he gladly cradled in his arms. "I see us growing more organically, from within," he said. "Starting with my son. There'll be more, I hope."

He liked the blush on Liberty's cheeks. "And it wouldn't hurt you, Zach, to contribute to the population explosion. Mikey could use playmates. Pepper, I'm not leaving you out, either."

"I have other things to work on, brother," Pepper said, and everyone leaned forward.

"Care to share?" Helen said. "We've been wondering since you returned to town and have been rather quiet."

Pepper got her purse. "I was a write-in to the sheriff's seat. That's not exactly quiet."

"But it's not like you, either. I remember the girl who was madly in love with—"

"No," Pepper said, breaking into Pansy's reminiscing. "Everything is in the past that should be."

"I own some empty land that could be used for a school," Holt said. "Unless you're going to be a rancher now, Zach."

Zach looked at his brother. "I guess I'll put the school on hold for now. My brother will need help at the Triple F. He can't run the sheriff's office, our ranch and be a new father."

"I thought you said he didn't do anything," Helen said lightly, and everyone patted Zach on the back. "Go ahead and surprise us with everything you want to do with your life, Zach. We forgive you for wanting to knock over our saloon."

"You know, it's not really a saloon," Zach said.

Duke said, "You're digging yourself in deep, brother. You might want to stop right there if you fancy living in this town. Trust me."

Zach grinned. "All right. It's a saloon." Sighing, he began to pack up his things, with a wink to Pansy and Helen. "Come on, Pepper. It looks like our job here is done."

Duke looked around the room, recognizing those sly looks on everyone's faces. "Don't tell me. You sent Pepper and Zach to take over my office so I'd have nothing to focus on except Liberty and my baby."

"Oh, no," Helen said, and everyone shook their heads a bit too innocently. "We would never plot against our favorite sheriff."

He was suspicious, because Zach and Pepper were just a little too happy to be leaving, and he thought he heard Zach tell Pepper, "Talk about a boring job!"

"Yeah, the paint didn't help as much as I thought it would. It's still a town office," Pepper said.

Duke gave his friends a hard look to let them know he wasn't deaf. "All right. Everyone out of my office. It's time for me to spend some time with my family. Until the next crisis, that is."

"Glad you're back, Sheriff," Mr. Parsons said. "Does that mean I can have my old cell back? And my dog?"

"Where is Molly-Jimbo?" Duke asked, and Pepper pointed to the pet who'd already made herself at home in the cell again. She slept in a basket lined with a plaid cushion.

Pepper smiled. "She liked it here. I couldn't bear to tell her to go. So we compromised, and I made her a proper bed."

"Thanks," Duke said gruffly, more pleased than he could say. "Now everyone depart. My son's hungry."

He waited until everyone filed out before giving Liberty a big kiss on the lips. "Are you sure about this?"

"My house is two blocks over, and I only walk the short end of those streets," she said. "It's less than five hundred feet. The baby will enjoy the stroll."

Duke nodded. "But at night—"

"At night we'll head home," Liberty said. "There's no place I'd rather be than at the Triple F with my sheriff."

"What changed your mind?"

Liberty looked at him. "I ran out of your life,

I plan on walking back into it knowing exactly who I am and that I will make you happy all your life."

Duke grabbed Liberty, pulling her to him. "My whole life is changing today," he said. "My townspeople, now you. I'm going to get quite the big head."

"You already had that," Liberty said, kissing Duke as they held their baby between them, "but I've got plenty of pins to pop you if it gets too big."

Duke looked down at her, loving her mischievous smile. "So will you marry me this time, Liberty Wentworth?"

"If you'll marry me, Duke Forrester." She smiled, her heart full for the first time in her life.

"And we have our own little ringbearer," Duke said, looking down at his son.

"Well, maybe he can be the pillow," Liberty said with a laugh. "Duke, he's going to be small for a long time."

"No," Duke said. "I can already tell he's got his mother's big heart." He gave Liberty the kiss he'd been waiting for more than a year to give her. "Surprise me and don't wear white. Hot mamas don't wear white." He didn't want to remember the first wedding, at least not the way he did. The future was his focus.

"Don't be scared, Duke. I'm not going anywhere this time." Liberty closed the office door and locked it, then put Mikey into his soft bassinet. "Let me show you how I intend to stay."

Duke grinned. Being married was going to be just his cup of tea.

Epilogue

Pink was the color Liberty settled on for her final wedding gown, this one so elegant and dream-come-true that two people had already asked her to duplicate the dress for their weddings. Liberty looked at Duke, so handsome and tall in his charcoal western wedding attire that her breath caught.

The ecstasy she'd always wanted to experience completely filled her heart.

Helen was her matron of honor, and Pansy and Pepper bridesmaids. Duke had insisted on a big wedding because, he said, he wanted everyone on the planet to know he'd finally caught her. Valentine, Hawk and Jellyfish from Union Junction brought out a stunning cake with lovely pink tulips cascading on the top.

"And people said I didn't like change," Duke

said, coming to give her a romantic kiss. "Seems like I've changed more than anybody in this town."

"I think the town changed as much as you did," Liberty said. "Anyway, you're still the most wonderful man I know."

"Liberty, if you keep talking like that, you're going to find yourself good and romanced," Duke said.

"I'd like that," she said. "I always dreamed of a day just like this one, Duke."

They held each other's hands for a long moment. "So, you're staying?" Duke said softly, his lips curved just a little into a smile.

"You couldn't run me off," she said, kissing those smiling lips. "I love you, Duke Forrester. You've always been the only man I could ever love, and being in love with you is…it's magic."

A baby wail drifted over to them, followed by lots of "Oohhss," meaning little Mikey was being spoiled rotten, so Liberty grabbed Duke's face, pulling him to her for a kiss that promised him everything he'd been denied before.

He grinned. "Now that's the way a wife should kiss her man."

Liberty smiled. "I was hoping you'd think that."

He nodded. "I'm very thankful and impressed,"

he said teasingly. "I can't wait to see how well you cook and clean, too."

"Duke!"

He laughed. "It's great to be the black sheep of the town."

"I have to know something," she said.

"That doesn't really surprise me," he said, his eyes twinkling as much as the beautiful diamond ring he'd given her yesterday. The diamonds surrounded by rubies reminded him of Tulips—a notion which Liberty loved.

"Helen and Pansy never gave you any kind of…recipe, did they?" she asked, looking up into his eyes.

Duke swept her up in his arms to walk toward their home together. "Recipe?" he said. "Like a recipe for winning your stubborn woman?"

She laughed and cradled her head against his chest. "Sounds like a recipe for winning your stubborn sheriff."

"So they got us both." He laughed. "Good for us."

Liberty smiled. It was better than good.

It was heaven.

* * * * *

Turn the page for a sneak preview of
THE CHRISTMAS TWINS, the second book in
Tina Leonard's miniseries
THE TULIPS SALOON,
coming November 2006
only from Harlequin American Romance!

Zach Forrester freely admitted that boredom was his worst enemy. He didn't mind living in Tulips, Texas, on the Triple F ranch, but he wanted to do more in his life than just take care of a family property. He had plans to build a new elementary school in the small town, a challenge he would enjoy.

But now it was time for a different challenge. Maybe the late September moon was getting to him, or maybe the fact that the girls he'd been casually dating had begun to seem a trifle silly, but excitement seemed to be a hard-to-find commodity.

One thing was for certain, he wasn't giving up his life the way Duke had, to diapers and a wife and a round-cheeked baby. He loved his little nephew, but a baby put a certain stop to one's life.

Nor would he ever let a woman lead him around by the nose as Liberty had Duke. She had left the altar with Duke standing at it, then come back pregnant with his baby, finally marrying Duke in a wonderfully romantic ceremony.

Of course, Duke was insanely happy with his new wife and child, but it had been hell on Duke getting there. Zach had to admit it had been fun watching his older brother struggle mightily to get his woman. *Everything always seems to come easy for Duke and Pepper and harder for me.*

He was enjoying his pity party as he drove, until he saw the hot pink convertible T-bird and the madwoman standing next to his favorite bull, which she'd clearly just hit. She was talking on her cell phone as if it was just any old piece of meat she'd struck. But that was Brahma Bud, his best and finest!

Hopping out of his truck, he stared at the imperious woman with whiskey-coloured hair. "What the hell do you think you're doing?"

She snapped her phone shut. "I am *trying* to get this beast to move, Cowboy," she said. "He seems to think he has the right of way."

"He does!" Zach stared at his poor bull, which gazed back in return, not bothered in the least by the annoying woman who had hit him.

"Well, he's been having his way for an hour," she replied, her voice so haughty it sounded like it belonged in New York. "Do you think you could move his plump hide?"

Perhaps Brahma Bud had only been lightly tapped, because the bull didn't seem any worse for the wear. He did, however, seem quite mesmerized by the pink T-bird, as was Zach himself. "What's the rush, City?"

"I have a life," she told him. "I just can't stand here and watch the grass grow."

Well, hell, Zach thought, wasn't she special. Of course, she certainly looked special in her tight dress. When she spoke, she emphasized her words so that all of her bounced in the right places. "He might move tomorrow," Zach said. "Once he gets to a spot he likes, he tends to stay there."

"You have *got* to be kidding me!" she exclaimed, enunciating and bouncing, to Zach's delight.

Ah, city folk. So much fun. He leaned against her T-bird and gave her his best leer. "When I get to a spot I like, I tend to stay there, too."

"Cowboy, I know all about guys like you, and believe me, the words are bigger than the deed. Just take your cow and go home, okay? And I won't charge you for the dent in my fender. Not to mention I think he used his antler to lift my skirt when I tried to make certain he was all right."

"Yeah, that would be the easy way out," Zach said slowly, realizing what he wanted more than anything was to shake things up, and this gal was a smoking-hot challenge even if she didn't know horns from antlers. "I'll do two things for you— one, I'll ask my prize longhorn here to move, if you're nice. Two, I won't ask why you're trespassing on my private drive, if you're nice. I won't even be mad that you hit my livelihood, here," he said, dropping a casual hand to Bud's horn. "However, I do insist upon a kiss."

Set in darkness beyond the ordinary world.
Passionate tales of life and death.
With characters' lives ruled by laws the everyday
world can't begin to imagine.

Introducing NOCTURNE, a spine-tingling
new line from Silhouette Books.

The thrills and chills begin with UNFORGIVEN
by Lindsay McKenna

Plucked from the depths of hell, former military sharpshooter Reno Manchahi was hired by the government to kill a thief, but he had a mission of his own. Descended from a family of shape-shifters, Reno vowed to get the revenge he'd thirsted for all these years. But his mission went awry when his target turned out to be a powerful seductress, Magdalena Calen Hernandez, who risked everything to battle a potent evil. Suddenly, Reno had to transform himself into a true hero and fight the enemy that threatened them all. He had to become a Warrior for the Light....

Turn the page for a sneak preview of
UNFORGIVEN by Lindsay McKenna.
On sale September 26, wherever books are sold.

Chapter 1

One shot...one kill.

The sixteen-pound sledgehammer came down with such fierce power that the granite boulder shattered instantly. A spray of glittering mica exploded into the air and sparkled momentarily around the man who wielded the tool as if it were a weapon. Sweat ran in rivulets down Reno Manchahi's drawn, intense face. Naked from the waist up, the hot July sun beating down on his back, he hefted the sledgehammer skyward once more. Muscles in his thick forearms leaped and biceps bulged. Even his breath was focused on the boulder. In his mind's eye, he pictured Army General Robert Hampton's fleshy, arrogant fifty-year-old features on the rock's surface. Air exploded from between his lips as he brought the avenging hammer down. The boulder pulverized beneath his funneled hatred.

One shot...one kill...

Nostrils flaring, he inhaled the dank, humid heat and drew it deep into his massive lungs. Revenge allowed Reno to endure his imprisonment at a U.S. Navy brig near San Diego, California. Drops of sweat were flung in all directions as the crack of his sledgehammer claimed a third stone victim. Mouth taut, Reno moved to the next boulder.

The other prisoners in the stone yard gave him a wide berth. They always did. They instinctively felt his simmering hatred, the palpable revenge in his cinnamon-colored eyes, was more than skin-deep.

And they whispered he was different.

Reno enjoyed being a loner for good reason. He came from a medicine family of shape-shifters. But even this secret power had not protected him—or his family. His wife, Ilona, and his three-year-old daughter, Sarah, were dead. Murdered by Army General Hampton in their former home on USMC base in Camp Pendleton, California. Bitterness thrummed through Reno as he savagely pushed the toe of his scarred leather boot against several smaller pieces of gray granite that were in his way.

The sun beat down upon Manchahi's naked shoulders, grown dark red over time, shouting his half-Apache heritage. With his straight black hair grazing his thick shoulders, copper skin and broad face with high cheekbones, everyone knew he was Indian. When he'd first arrived at the brig, some of the prisoners taunted him and called him Geronimo. Something strange happened to Reno during his fight with the name-calling prisoners. Leaning down after he'd won the scuffle, he'd snarled into each of their bloodied faces that if they were going to call him anything, they would call him *gan,* which was the Apache word for *devil.*

His attackers had been shocked by the wounds on their faces, the deep claw marks. Reno recalled doubling his fist as they'd attacked him en masse. In that split second, he'd gone into an altered state of consciousness. In times of danger, he transformed into a jaguar. A deep, growling sound had emitted from his throat as he defended himself in the three-against-one fracas. It all happened so fast that he thought he had imagined it. He'd seen his hands morph into a forearm and paw, claws extended. The slashes left on the three men's faces after the fight told him he'd begun to shape-shift. A fist made bruises and swelling; not four perfect, deep claw marks. Stunned and anxious, he hid the knowledge of what else he was from these prisoners. Reno's only defense was to make all the prisoners so damned scared of him and remain a loner.

Alone. Yeah, he was alone, all right. The steel hammer swept downward with hellish ferocity. As the granite groaned in protest, Reno shut his eyes for just a moment. Sweat dripped off his nose and square chin.

Straightening, he wiped his furrowed, wet brow and looked into the pale blue sky. What got his attention was the startling cry of a red-tailed hawk as it flew over the brig yard. Squinting, he watched the bird. Reno could make out the rust-colored tail on the hawk. As a kid growing up on the Apache reservation in Arizona, Reno knew that all animals that appeared before him were messengers.

Brother, what message do you bring me? Reno knew one had to ask in order to receive. Allowing the sledgehammer to drop to his side, he concentrated on the hawk who wheeled in tightening circles above him.

Freedom! the hawk cried in return.

Reno shook his head, his black hair moving against his broad, thickset shoulders. *Freedom? No way, Brother. No way.* Figuring that he was making up the hawk's shrill message, Reno turned away. Back to his rocks. Back to picturing Hampton's smug face.

Freedom!

* * * * *

Look for UNFORGIVEN by Lindsay McKenna,
the spine-tingling launch title from
Silhouette Nocturne™.
Available September 26, wherever books are sold.

SAVE UP TO $30! SIGN UP TODAY!

INSIDE Romance

The complete guide to your favorite
Harlequin®, Silhouette® and Love Inspired® books.

✓ Newsletter ABSOLUTELY FREE! No purchase necessary.

✓ Valuable coupons for future purchases of Harlequin,
Silhouette and Love Inspired books in every issue!

✓ Special excerpts & previews in each issue. Learn about all
the hottest titles before they arrive in stores.

✓ No hassle—mailed directly to your door!

✓ Comes complete with a handy shopping checklist
so you won't miss out on any titles.

- -

SIGN ME UP TO RECEIVE INSIDE ROMANCE
ABSOLUTELY FREE
(Please print clearly)

_____
Name

_____
Address

_____
City/Town   State/Province   Zip/Postal Code

(098 KKM EJL9)

Please mail this form to:
In the U.S.A.: Inside Romance, P.O. Box 9057, Buffalo, NY 14269-9057
In Canada: Inside Romance, P.O. Box 622, Fort Erie, ON L2A 5X3
OR visit http://www.eHarlequin.com/insideromance

IRNBPA06R   ® and ™ are trademarks owned and used by the trademark owner and/or its licensee.

IOA

**If you enjoyed what you just read,
then we've got an offer you can't resist!**

Take 2 bestselling
love stories FREE!

Plus get a FREE surprise gift!

Clip this page and mail it to Harlequin Reader Service®

IN U.S.A.
3010 Walden Ave.
P.O. Box 1867
Buffalo, N.Y. 14240-1867

IN CANADA
P.O. Box 609
Fort Erie, Ontario
L2A 5X3

YES! Please send me 2 free Harlequin American Romance® novels and my free surprise gift. After receiving them, if I don't wish to receive anymore, I can return the shipping statement marked cancel. If I don't cancel, I will receive 4 brand-new novels every month, before they're available in stores! In the U.S.A., bill me at the bargain price of $4.24 plus 25¢ shipping & handling per book and applicable sales tax, if any*. In Canada, bill me at the bargain price of $4.99 plus 25¢ shipping & handling per book and applicable taxes**. That's the complete price and a savings of at least 10% off the cover prices—what a great deal! I understand that accepting the 2 free books and gift places me under no obligation ever to buy any books. I can always return a shipment and cancel at any time. Even if I never buy another book from Harlequin, the 2 free books and gift are mine to keep forever.

154 HDN DZ7S
354 HDN DZ7T

Name	(PLEASE PRINT)	
Address	Apt.#	
City	State/Prov.	Zip/Postal Code

Not valid to current Harlequin American Romance® subscribers.

Want to try two free books from another series?
Call 1-800-873-8635 or visit www.morefreebooks.com.

* Terms and prices subject to change without notice. Sales tax applicable in N.Y.
** Canadian residents will be charged applicable provincial taxes and GST.
   All orders subject to approval. Offer limited to one per household.
   ® are registered trademarks owned and used by the trademark owner and or its licensee.

AMER04R   ©2004 Harlequin Enterprises Limited